The *Killer* Monument

CHARLES W. GARNACHE

Thank you for being good friends.

[signature]

Gulf of Maine Publishing

Cover designed by Christina Garnache

This book is published by arrangement with
Gulf of Maine Publishing
West St. , First Floor
Biddeford, ME 04005

Printed in Maine, United States of America

To Kathy
with love

FORWARD

This novel brings together the several legends, mysteries, and superstitions prevalent in the Biddeford Pool and Saco River area prior to World War II.

Although written as fiction, the knowledgeable reader will not find it difficult to recognize the setting and some of the events. Of course, any similarity between persons living or dead is purely coincidental.

This is a fast-moving, action-packed thriller that will hold the reader's interest by the quality of work, rather than an appeal to one's most base instincts. Though directed toward young adult readers, persons of all ages will find it enjoyable.

The author has won recognition in international competition sponsored by Writer's Digest and is the recipient of the Horatio Bunce Award for his essays on liberty.

TABLE OF CONTENTS

INTRODUCTION

While sailing up the Saco River, some English explorers saw an Indian woman with her baby crossing the river in a canoe. They wondered if the infant of a "savage" could swim like a newborn dog or cat. The explorers took the infant from its mother and threw it into the water. The mother, screaming in grief over the loss of her baby, cursed the sailors - "Three white men will drown in the Saco every year, forevermore!" And, as the curse held true year after year, it came to pass that a cloud of fear and superstition dominated the culture of the settlements at the mouth of the Saco. The object of greatest trepidation was the monument on Stage Island that strangely resembled a teepee. Nobody knew when or how it came into being!

The *Killer* Monument

"Twist, Turn & Burn!"

Chapter I

It was the end of June, 1941. Jim Collins stood on the beach near his home. He looked out over the water toward Stage Island studying the monument that stood on it.

As Claudine Grant, his next door neighbor, ran down the path toward him, she shouted his name excitedly. "Look at what I found between the pages of an old book!" she said. "It's an article from the Journal dated August 2, 1901." Claudine held the yellowed newspaper clipping in front of Jim. "Listen. I'll read it to you:

ONE OF THE MOST PROMINENT OBJECTS
NEXT TO WOOD ISLAND LIGHTHOUSE,
THAT ATTRACTS THE ATTENTION OF THE
STRANGER STANDING ALMOST ANYWHERE
ON THE GREAT SEMI-CIRCLE WHICH SWINGS
INLAND FROM THE MOUTH OF THE SACO
AND OUTWARD AGAIN TO STOUT NECK,

IS THE TALL CONICAL GRAY STONE TOWER
ON STAGE ISLAND.

NO OTHER OBJECT THAT STRIKES THE EYE
IS MORE INQUIRED UPON THAN THIS TALL
STONE STRUCTURE, AND NONE ABOUT
WHICH SO LITTLE IS KNOWN. WHO BUILT IT,
WHEN AND FOR WHAT PURPOSE WAS IT
ERECTED, CONSTITUTE A STANDING PUZZLE,
UPON WHICH SCARCELY ANY OF THOSE BORN
AND REARED WITHIN SIGHT OF THE
STRUCTURE, CAN SHED A RAY OF LIGHT. THE
IMPRESSION HAS BEEN GENERAL THAT IT IS A
RELIC OF ANTIQUITY, DATING BACK PERHAPS
TWO HUNDRED YEARS OR MORE; AND THIS
SUPPOSITION HAS LENT ADDED INTEREST TO
THE MYSTERIOUS CONE AND GIVEN RISE TO
MUCH CURIOUS SPECULATION AS TO ITS
PROBABLE ORIGIN.

"What do you think of that, huh?"

"Let me see it." Jim read the article to himself. "It doesn't tell us anything." he said shaking his head.

"What do you mean? Of course it tells us something. Now we know it must have been built before 1700 when about the only people living around here were Indians, and nobody else knows any more about it than we do. It also tells us that if we're going to get the answers, we're going to have to go out there and get them ourselves."

"Like I said, Claud. It doesn't tell us a thing."

"Well, it's a start."

"Sure! A start to nowhere! What I'd like to know is when did the legend start that no one has ever set foot in that monument and survived. I'd like to know who started it and why. Than we'd be getting somewhere."

Claudine looked at Jim, annoyed. "What difference does that make? You've said a hundred times that those stories are nothing but superstition."

"Yes, they're superstitions, all right, but somebody must've had a reason for starting them. What's out there that somebody wanted to make sure nobody ever saw or found out?"

"Well that's what we're going to find out ourselves, right?"

"Not so fast, Claud. There's a lot of things we have to do before we can even think of going out there."

"Like what?"

"Like making money this summer, for one thing."

"You know, Jim, I just don't understand you. We've been years waiting for the chance to get out to that island, and now you don't act interested."

As Claudine spoke, Jim looked down at his right hand. First he held it palm up, then he turned it over to look at the back of it. His attention was on the stub where his index finger should have been. Now he held it out for Claudine to see. "This is what my curiosity cost me once, not to mention the dozens of times we've both been in trouble around here because we just had to know. Now this time we could really get ourselves in over our heads." He paused for a moment and sat down on the sandy beach. Claudine sat down beside him. He pointed to the water's edge. "This isn't like the time you spent a month lying on this beach to figure out why the gulls stamped their feet as the water came in across the sand. This is serious! We've got to weigh the chances of success against the possibility of getting hurt."

"True. But look at what we learned that time. You and I know that an animal with a brain as small as a seagull's can actually learn something, by itself, that goes beyond what it knows by instinct. Just think of the implications of that!"

"I have, plenty of times. But who cares?"

"We do!" she said.

"Yes, we do, don't we?" Jim felt excitement build up inside him. "You're right! That's what really counts. Okay, let's go home and get ready to go clamming tomorrow, and then we can start making plans."

That evening Jim found it difficult to sleep. Thoughts of the strange village of Stout Neck, his home, kept flashing into his mind.

There was the rickety Sidebottom house that leaned toward the sea like it was about to fall into it with the jaw bones of a huge whale forming an archway that guarded the entrance. At night the place looked like a monster to Jim, ready to pounce on anyone who came within reach of its jaws.

Then there was the abandoned Callahan place. It had been an inn for sailors and assorted cutthroats. In his mind, Jim saw the men who had been drugged and dragged unconscious to some waiting ship to sail the seven seas against their will.

He knew the legends of Indians and pirates. There was the strange stone fort at Wooded Point where no fort should have been and no fort on Fort Hill where a fort should have stood.

The tales of rum runners and sunken ships were enough by themselves to keep Jim's imagination exploding forever.

To Jim, even the pine trees looked scared. Their trunks and limbs were twisted out of shape as if they were trying to hide from someone or something.

He had been told it was because of the wind that swept across the peninsula that made the trees look the way they did. That sounded good to him except he realized the trees on the other peninsulas didn't look tortured like those.

Claudine was his best friend. Everybody called her "Claud" which was a little confusing to him. He thought it would be better if he started calling her "Claudine" even though she could do anything he tried to do, and usually did. They were such close friends, they celebrated their birthdays with the same party.

In all of Stout Neck, Claudine was the only person Jim knew who didn't have a look of fear or impending doom The mood of the people of Stout Neck puzzled Jim more than

CLAM FORK (DIGGER) and CLAM BASKET

anything else.

With that his thoughts slipped from view and he fell asleep.

Early the next morning Jim and Claudine walked to the shore of Back Bay. A heavy fog hid everything from view. Jim rowed the skiff to their favorite spot, and they began to dig for clams.

The bay was about two miles wide and three miles long. At low tide, the only water in the bay was a narrow channel that went the length of the bay and another that crossed it. At high tide, the bay was flooded to many feet in depth.

The place where they were digging was on the side of a high bog of wet spongy ground covered with marsh grass. Jim looked up from his work toward Claudine. "Do you like being called 'Claud'?"

"That's my name, isn't it?"

"I know, but 'Claud' is a boy's name. I've got an uncle named Claud. It seems strange to me that your parents would give you a nickname like that."

"Isn't everything strange around here?"

"Yeah, it sure is, but 'Claud' is still a boy's name."

"Well, I think it's a good name. I can do anything you can, so what's wrong with my name?"

"Nothing! It's just now that we're grown up, I thought you might like it better if I called you 'Claudine'"

"Well, we're not really grown up, and 'Claud' is fine by me." She straightened up from her stooped position and stared toward the bog. "Hey! Listen! Do you hear that? It sounds like somebody is fighting on the other side of the bog."

"Let's go see."

"I'm way ahead of you." She charged toward the tall grass.

"Keep your head down," Jim warned.

As they crawled through the grass the sounds of a struggle were heard more clearly. By parting the grass they saw two men fighting with their clam hoes.

Claudine stared wide-eyed at the four ten-inch steel blades one of the men tried to drive into the body of the other. Because the blades were at a hundred-degree angle to the eighteen inch handle the attacker swung it in an arc like a tennis player hitting a ball. The other man held his out-stretched in front of him in an attempt to keep the first man away and to block his blows.

"They're going to kill each other!" Claudine gasped.

"Quiet! You want them to see us?" Jim warned.

"One of the men was tall, lean and over six feet tall. The other was about five foot, six. The little man had wild brown hair. A gray stubble of hair covered his bony cheeks. He was wearing a long coat that almost reached his ankles. The leather belt around his waist was two feet too -long. The extra length hung below his knees. In his left hand he held a lunch box. It was held closed by another leather belt that was also too long.

The little man actually attacked the big man. He swung with his clam digger. The tall man blocked the attack with his own digger then the smaller man smashed him with his lunch box.

The big man shouted with pain. "I'll kill ya, Baby

THE BACK BAY AT LOW TIDE SHROUDED IN FOG

Bum! If ya don't get out of here, I'll kill ya!"

Baby Bum shouted right back at him, "This is my spot! You get out!"

"First come, first serve," the tall man yelled as he caught a hard blow to his ribs from the lunch box.

"Everybody's always trying to cheat me out of what's mine," Baby Bum screamed. "You get out of here or I'll kill you!"

"The clam flats don't belong to you, you idiot," argued the tall man as he caught another blow to his battered ribs.

Baby Bum's arms swung in every direction with the swiftness of a bird's wings. Finally, the big man knocked him to the ground with a powerful kick to the stomach.

He lay in the mud groaning in pain. The tall man stood over him. "That'll teach ya to mess with me, Baby Bum. Ya try that again, and the next time I'll drive ya into the ground deeper than the clams!" Apparently convinced he had won the battle the tall man walked back to where he was digging, stooped over and began to work.

Jim and Claudine lay motionless in the tall grass. They watched Baby Bum, wondering how badly he was hurt. Neither knew what to do. Before they decided on a course of action they noticed baby Bum's body relax. Then he lifted his head a couple of inches and looked toward the tall man. The tall man was still stooped over with his back to him.

Baby Bum got to his feet. Quickly and silently he approached his enemy. At about six feet from him he raised his digger high over his head, took another step and drove the digger into the tall man's back.

The wounded man dropped face first into the mud. His body began twitching and turning every which way. The single blow killed him, throwing his body into death spasms. Baby Bum while in a crouched position jumped up and down, always facing the twisting body, and screamed in delight. "Twist, turn and burn!" he yelled over and over as he circled his victim.

Claudine gasped and clasped her hand over her mouth.

"Shhhh," Jim cautioned frantically.

"He killed him!"

"Be quiet! I think he heard you! He's looking this way!"

Claudine started to turn toward the other side of the bog. "Let's get out of here!"

"No! If we move, he'll see the grass shake and then he'll know we're here. Lie still," he warned. "Don't move a muscle. We'll wait until he's gone, if he hasn't seen us already."

She looked back toward the scene of the struggle. "What's he doing now? Why is he standing on him!"

Jim looked at Claudine with disbelief. "He's trying to pull the digger out of the dead man's back!"

"He's crazy!"

"Of course he's crazy! Sane people don't go around killing each other over a few clams!"

Baby Bum took everything of any value from his vic-

SOUTH SIDE OF THE THATCH BED AS SEEN FROM THE POOL

tim including his clams. He loaded his boat and rowed away.

"He's not going up the channel!" Jim said fearfully. "He's rowing toward our boat! He's going to spot it for sure!"

"Come on! Let's get there first."

"Stay down," he ordered. "If he sees our boat, we're not going to be able to get by him anyway. If we go up the channel, we'll be trapped. The only way out is through him!"

"Maybe the fog is thick enough to hide our boat."

"I don't think so. We'd better get back to the other side like you suggested. We'll be able to see what he's doing better from over there."

"That's what I was trying to tell you. The end of the bog is blocking our view from here."

They crawled as carefully as they could trying not to give their position away by disturbing the grass. Claudine was the first one to reach the other side. "Look! He's turning up the other channel. He's moving away from us!"

"No, he isn't! He's stopping! He's seen our boat!" Jim ducked lower in the grass.

"What do we do now?" she whispered.

"Let's just stay put. Don't even breathe until we're sure of what he's going to do. If he comes this way we'll

have to make a run for it across the flats."

"But we can't do that! We'll get trapped in the mud! Nobody has ever gotten through the soft muck in the center of the flats!"

"We're going to have to try if he comes after us. You saw what a maniac he is!"

She looked at Jim intently. "If we get caught in the mud in this fog, nobody will be able to see us. We'll drown when the tide comes in!"

"Quiet! Here he comes!"

They watched as Baby Bum began to row slowly toward their boat. He scowled, straining to see if anyone was around. He beached his skiff and started to get out.

"It's time for us to retreat. Keep your head down," Jim warned.

They crawled to the other side, got to their feet and began running across the flats. "This will give us a head start anyway," Claudine said as she ran alongside Jim.

After about a hundred yards, Jim stopped. "Okay, this is far enough." He turned and looked toward the bog. "I

FOOTPRINTS LEADING TO A QUAGMIRE

can barely see the grass. If we stand perfectly still we should be able to see him before he can spot us."

"Jim! We forgot our diggers! We don't have a thing to protect ourselves with!"

"I know. We had no way of knowing we'd need them."

Claudine grabbed Jim's arm. "There he is! Can you see him?"

"Yes. He's just looking around."

"How come he looks so huge?"

"It's the fog. It makes everything look bigger for some reason or other."

"Oh, God! Here he comes!" she whispered.

"Think ya can fool Baby Bum, do ya? I know ya're out there. Ya think I'm too dumb to see footprints, huh? Git ready to meet yaw maker 'cause I'm comin' to git ya!"

"We've got no choice now." Jim grabbed Claudine's hand and started to run. "Let's hope we can make it across the mud."

They had run about three-quarters of a mile when they came to the soft clay-type mud in the center of the flats. It became increasingly difficult to move. With each step they sank deeper. As its grip got stronger they got weaker.

Baby Bum closed his distance to less than twenty yards. He waved the murderess clam digger in the air while all the time screaming threats of death. In his other hand was the steel lunch box which he had used on his previous victim.

His oversized coat was dragging in the mud along with the end of his leather belt that kept it gathered tightly around his waist. To Jim, his hate-filled eyes and his wild brown hair made him look more terrible than anything in a nightmare.

Claudine reached out and caught Jim's arm. Only her eyes pleaded for help. Her lungs were too desperate for air to spare enough for her to utter a single word.

The mud held their feet firmly. They could not take another step. Baby Bum shook with delight. "I got ya now. Thought ya could make trouble for me, did ya? Well you brats ain't gonna make trouble for nobody nomore!"

Jim and Claudine twisted their bodies so they could see Baby Bum. Holding on to Claudine for balance, Jim raised his free hand in a sign for him to stop.

"Wait a minute!" Jim gasped.

"What for?" Baby Bum screamed through clenched teeth.

"You'll get stuck like us," Jim managed to say between gulps of air.

"Ya think I'm stupid like you brats? I ain't got no intention of going in that muck. I ain't gonna have to kill ya. The tide will do that for me." His laughter sent chills over their bodies. "It won't be long now. Ya feel the crabs nibbling at yaw toes yet? Ya don't? Pretty quick now ya will. Crabs love to eat people...dead or alive!"

They began to shake with terror. "Don't try to move," Jim advised between chattering teeth. "save your strength."

"I'm gonna leave ya now. Them crabs are gonna have a nice meal on yaw young and tender bodies! He turned and started back toward the bog.

"When he's out of sight, you try to pull yourself out by holding on to me," Jim said with desperation.

"I'll try, but I doubt if it will do any good. We've both sunk even deeper since we've stopped!"

"Okay, okay! Let's take a minute to get our heads together. If we don't panic, I'm sure we can get out of this mess." He was trying to comfort himself as much as Claudine.

"Look at the tide! It's coming in faster than ever! I've never seen it come in that fast!"

"Take it easy! For crying out loud, take it easy! It only seems that way. As near as I can figure, we've got an hour and a half before the water will be over our heads."

Claudine screamed, "There's a crab!"

"Stop it! You'll have us both in a state of panic if you keep that up. The crabs are the least of our problems for the time being."

"Oh, no!" Claudine moaned.

"Wha-what's the matter now?"

"What if Baby Bum comes back in his boat? We'll be at his mercy!"

It's In The Wrong Place

Chapter II

Jim looked at Claudine. The color began draining from his face. He shook his head violently. "Let's not even think about that. Let's concentrate on getting out of this mud." As he twisted his body toward her, he told her to hold on to him and try to get herself out.

The fast rising tide was now up to their waists. When Jim guessed how much time they had to free themselves he forgot to consider they were already knee-deep in mud.

Claudine did the best she could to break loose form the mud's grip. After several minutes she was exhausted. "I think I have a better idea," she gasped.

"What is it?"

"You try to get yourself out by holding on to me. If you do, then you can help get me out."

"But I'm stronger than you," he protested. "We've

better chance of getting you out first."

"You are not stronger than me, but you are taller, so you can reach me better. Just put your weight on me and try to get your legs unstuck. If you can then lay behind me in the water and I'll try to get out by sitting on you."

Jim twisted his body so as to be able to put as much weight on Claudine as possible. She was on his left which meant he had to try to get his right leg out first.

Claudine strained under his weight. Struggling for a few minutes, he felt his leg move a little. "It's working! Yes, I'm sure it's working! My leg is almost out! That's it! It's out!"

"Be careful!" she shouted. "Don't knock us over or we'll be in worse trouble than we are now."

Jim fought to regain his balance. Finally with his free leg behind him, he was able to steady his shaking body. He leaned more heavily on Claudine. As he pulled on his left leg to get it free his weight began forcing her into the water. He pushed with his right leg to take some of the pressure off her. His right leg was stuck again.

"This isn't going to work!" he cried in frustration.

"Wait a minute, Jim. Just calm down. Get your right leg out again then put it behind you and sit on it. Then maybe we can get the other one out by both of us pulling on it."

He leaned on Claudine. In another minute he had the right leg free. He folded his leg under him and tried to sit on it. "I can't do it," he moaned.

"Why not?"

"Because I'm not a girl! I can't bend it that far."

"Well kneel on it then. That'll be even better."

Jim did as she suggested. He reached into the water and began scooping mud away from his trapped leg. When he had enough of it cleared away to get a good grip on his leg, he and Claudine began pulling and twisting it. In his kneeling position the water touched his chin. Within an instant he felt his leg give a little. For a moment he wasn't sure, but with the next effort he was positive. "It's coming!"

he shouted. "It's coming real good!"

Jim struggled with renewed enthusiasm. The promise of success gave him greater strength. Still the mud held giving up its grip but one inch at a time. Finally, he pulled his leg from the mud.

"I'm out! I'm free!" he shouted. But his joy quickly turned to doubt and fear. Although he shivered from the cold water, beads of sweat formed on his forehead. He felt his heart pound in his chest. The water was now too deep to help Claudine without having to put his head underwater. He knew time was running out for her.

He would have to go underwater for Claudine to sit on him to get herself free, and he knew there was no way he could hold his breath that long. Only her head and shoulders were out of the water.

Without saying a word, he ducked under the water and began to dig frantically around her leg. Even underwater he felt her body shake. As he dug he felt a clam shell cut deeply into one of his fingers. He ignored the wound and kept digging until he could no longer hold his breath. He bobbed his head out of the water, snapped his mouth open and sucked air in one prolonged gasp until he was able to get control of his lungs. He filled them with air and dropped below the surface.

To his horror he found the mud filled the hole as fast as he emptied it, but then he noticed it was loose where he had dug and didn't grip the leg as firmly as before.

As he felt the need for air coming on he forced his hands down along Claudine's leg as far as he could, reaching her ankle. He placed his knees on either side of her leg. While gripping her ankle with all his strength, he pulled with all his might. Slowly at first, and then with a jerk the leg broke free of the mud.

With the release of her leg, he turned his face toward the surface. His diaphragm and his lungs were about to force him to breathe. As his upturned face broke water, he popped his mouth open even as the water still ran off it. The air rushed into his lungs in a long mournful sigh. As he struggled to get control of his breathing, he saw that Claudine would soon be trapped under the surface. The fast rising tide had now covered her shoulders.

He decided on one final and desperate gamble. Either they would both survive, or both drown. There was time for only one more attempt. Between gasps of air he said, "I'm going to dig around your other leg. Then when I signal by hitting your shin with my knuckles, you stand on my back with your free foot and push."

Once again he dropped to the bottom to scoop mud away from her leg. This time he used both hands. He positioned himself flat on the bottom. He tapped her shin and felt her foot settle between his shoulder blades in response. Her weight pressed down upon him. He reached with his left hand and pulled. His breathe was being squeezed out of him. By the pressure of Claudine's foot on his back he could tell she was having difficulty keeping her balance. Even so, he felt the leg inch up through the mud.

He began to feel the need for air under his breast bone. Slowly the sensation moved to the pit of his stomach. His brain began protesting the frustration of its command. It was a feeling akin to panic; but unlike panic, there was a strange painful sensation in his head and diaphragm.

Claudine's leg broke from the mud's grip just as he lost control of his breathing. Her weight was suddenly released from his body. He tasted the salt of the ocean as it rushed into his opened mouth. His head shot above the surface. He felt a valve in his throat close.

No air could pass in or out of his lungs. He struggled to make a sound, but could not. No matter how hard he tried he couldn't breathe. He looked at Claudine. He strained to open his eyes wider in a plea for help. His face twisted and distorted from the pain as the muscles in his stomach felt like they were being torn apart.

Claudine looked at Jim with fear in her eyes not understanding what was happening to him. She begged him to tell her what was wrong over and over again.

Just as Jim started to feel dizzy he felt a trickle of air leak into his lungs. He coughed once, weakly, and then was able to breathe more freely. He made loud, squeaky, rasping sounds as he tried to inhale that sent chills all over Claudine's body. "What's happening?" she asked.

"I don't know," he gasped. "Let's just get out of here, fast."

They were just within reach of the opposite shore when Claudine cried out, "Here he comes!"

Jim turned his head to see Baby Bum rowing his boat toward them. "Don't worry about him. He can't catch us now."

They ran the remaining distance to the shore before Baby Bum could reach them. Jim turned and shouted at him, "You better get out of here, creep. We're going to call the cops. Besides, there isn't any way you can catch us now."

"Ya go ahead and call the cops," Baby Bum yelled back. "Tain't gonna do ya any good. Ain't nobody can catch me. But ya watch, I'll fix you brats. I'll sneak into yaw house some night and kill ya both in yaw sleep."

They ran up the road that followed the shore. Instead of going to their homes, they went right to the constable's house. The village of Stout Neck wasn't big enough to support a police department, so one of the fisherman served as the town constable. He opened the door in response to their knock.

Jim and Claudine blurted out the story of what they had seen.

"Now wait a minute. Just wait one minute, now," the constable said impatiently. "One at a time. Now you, Jim, describe this character for me."

"Yes! He was a little less than five and a half feet tall, a hundred to a hundred and thirty pounds. It was hard to tell with his overcoat on..."

"Wait a minute there," the constable interrupted Jim. "An overcoat! On the clam flats?"

"Yes, sir. He had a big old overcoat that went almost down to his feet, and it was held around his middle with a leather belt that was too long. Just like the one that kept his lunch box closed..."

"A lunch box! You mean while he was chasing you two, he was carrying a lunch box!" The constable was wide-eyed with disbelief.

"Yes, sir. Like we said, he used it as a weapon," Claudine said. "And we heard the murdered man call him by name, Baby Bum."

"Baby what!"

"Baby Bum," Claudine repeated.

"Baby Bum, huh," the constable repeated sarcastically. "Now you two kids listen to me. I know you two have pretty wild imaginations. I've seen the two of you poking around this village ever since you were toddlers, sticking your noses everywhere but where they belong. Always pestering people with silly questions that ain't none of your concern. Like that monument, for instance.

"But when you come to the police with a wild story like you just told me, you can get yourselves into a pecko' trouble." He raised his finger in warning, pointing at them. "Now you run on home and don't be bothering people with your fairy tales."

"But..."

"No but's about it," he shouted. "Now run along."

They looked at each other, shrugged their shoulders and stepped off the porch. "Well, what do we do now?" Claudine asked as they started to walk home.

"I don't know. Let's try to think the way the killer would."

"How can we think like a crazy man?"

"Well, look at the things he said to us, about the crabs eating us and his sneaking into our rooms at night to kill us in our sleep. He might be crazy, but he's not stupid. He said those things to scare us into doing something stupid."

"Sure! Why not? He was trying to panic us. And if

we had fallen for it, we'd both have drowned!" Claudine stared into the distance. She thought for a moment. "So do you think he'll forget about us and skip this part of the country?"

"I think so. I know I would, wouldn't you?"

"I would. But I don't think he will."

"Why not?" he asked.

"Because of the things he said when he was fighting the other man. He kept insisting it was his spot the other man was digging in. He acted like he owned the place. So we know he's crazy and if he thinks he owns the place, he's not about to leave it. Then he kills a man and accuses us of making trouble. The way I see it, he most likely thinks he did the right thing and was only protecting what is his."

"I don't know. You might be right," he agreed. "Anyway there's a good chance he'll decide to clear out, but to be on the safe side, we won't do anything or go anywhere unless we're together or we've got someone else with us. But we shouldn't say anything to our parents. They most likely won't believe us either."

"Okay," Claudine agreed. "But how are we going to explain the fact we don't have any clams or our boat?"

"We don't have to say anything to anybody yet. We'll take the dory and go get our boat. Then we'll worry about the rest of it."

"Good idea! With two of us rowing we'll stand a better chance against Baby Bum if we run into him."

They dropped down off the beach road and walked the rest of the way to the dory following the shore. When they got to the boat Jim took the forward rowing position, and Claudine the aft station.

As they leaned on the oars the dory glided over the flat, calm water. The two pairs of oars moved with precision in the expert hands of Jim and Claudine. The movement of their arms and bodies was synchronized as perfectly as a professional dance team.

Arriving at the spot where they had left their boat they

looked on all sides. For a moment neither dared state the obvious until Claudine said in a half-whisper, "It's not here."

Jim kept his voice down to a hush as if he sensed someone was nearby. "None of our things are here either!"

"What do you think, Jim?"

"Baby Bum is what I think."

"So, now what do we do?"

"Get some ammunition, I guess."

"Ammunition?" Claudine looked at Jim with a frown.

"Rocks," he said. "Let's go ashore and pick up a bunch of good throwing rocks."

"Hey! Good idea! You and I could hold off an army with a bunch of good throwing rocks."

Once the stones were loaded on board they rowed along the shore hoping it was the current and not Baby Bum that took their boat from where they had left it.

Although the bay was only three miles long and two miles wide, it was many miles along the shore. They had covered half the distance when Claudine was overcome by a feeling of isolation. The only thing visible was the deserted shore line and the flat, calm water for a hundred yards. Everything else was hidden by the dense fog.

She turned her head slowly looking around the dory trying to see through the fog. She had an awed expression. "It's like we're the only two people in the whole world and this little patch of water is the whole world," she told Jim. "This sure is a strange place. With all the mysteries we have around here, now we have a murder!"

"Yeah, but it's that monument that's driving me crazy," Jim admitted. "I wish this Baby Bum thing would just blow away so we could try to solve that one."

"Me, too," she agreed. "I don't understand why everybody is so scared of the place. Nobody says so, but just mention the monument, and right away they try to change the subject."

I know. I think it's because they don't know anything about it," he suggested. "So they've imagined all kinds of things.

You know how grown-ups are. They don't like to admit to kids that there's something they know nothing about."

"My father said it was built to mark a channel, but that doesn't make any sense. Why would a monument be built that's bigger than the lighthouse and on an island behind it?"

"Exactly right! And if it was built to guide ships then it's in the wrong place. And what about the story that anyone entering the monument will never be seen again?"

"Do you believe that?" she asked.

"You know I don't. But what about the gulls? There are thousands of them guarding the island!"

"Oh, Jim, they're most likely just guarding their chicks. That has to be why there are so many of them. It's because they nest there."

"Yeah, well how come they don't nest on any of the other islands?"

"I have to admit that is strange."

"Well, I know where we can get some answers about this place and that's from Mr. Sidebottom. Would you be game to go there?"

"Why should he be able to tell us anything?" she argued.

"Because he's so old he can even remember when there were still Indians around here. He could tell us about the fort and the Callahan place, too, I'll bet."

"His place is spookier than the monument and the Callahan place," she protested.

"I suppose. Well, if you don't want to, we won't."

"Oh, I know. You think I'm scared, don't you?"

"No. Not really. If you don't think we should go then let's forget it."

"Well, I think it's a good idea. So, the first chance we get, we're going," Claudine insisted.

"That's settled then, right?"

"Right. It's settled."

As they talked they searched the shore. Because of their positions at the oars Jim talked to the back of Claudine's head. She stopped rowing and turned in her seat so she could see him. "You know, we've just about covered this entire shoreline and still no boat."

Jim looked around slowly, putting off as long as he could, facing up to what was nagging at him the whole time. "Well, I guess we'd better head for Indian Cove. If we don't find it there we'll have to wait until the fog lifts and give it another try."

Claudine made a face like she tasted something she didn't like. "Of course you know the only way it could get in there is if someone took it there. I mean a boat can't drift against the tide, right?"

"Yeah, I know. That's what I don't like about it."

A few minutes later they arrived at the entrance to the cove. They stopped rowing and let the boat glide slowly into it while they watched the shore on each side of the dory slip by.

"There it is!" Jim whispered nervously.

"I don't see anybody, do you?"

"No." Jim placed his oars in the water stopping the forward progress of the boat. "Let's back into shore. That way we'll be able to get out fast if we have to. When we get there, I'll get out and untie our boat. You be ready with the rocks. If he shows, you start throwing. Just make sure you don't bean me while you're at it!"

"I won't hit you," she protested. "I'm just as good a shot as you. Be careful," she warned. "An army could hide behind those bushes."

Jim pointed the stern toward the shore pushing gently on the oars. The dory moved slowly, gradually taking away their margin of safety.

Claudine stood behind him by the forward rowing position with a rock the size of a large egg in each hand. She stared intently at the line of bushes that grew twenty feet from the beach.

"See anything?" Jim whispered.

"No." From her standing position she could see inside their skiff. "Hey, look! All of our stuff is in it!"

With one final push on the oars the dory hit the beach. Within an instant Jim jumped out and grabbed the anchor line. The moment he took his gaze from the bushes he heard Claudine scream, "Look out! There he is!"

He snapped his head up. He was still in a crouch position as he saw Baby Bum charging at him from ten feet away.

A steady scream came from Baby Bum's throat. He held the clam digger high in the air in his right hand. The steel lunch box was in the other, extended as far out as he could reach. His next two strides put him within striking distance of Jim.

Jim's body was still in a crouch looking upward to keep the clam digger in view. As Baby Bum started to drive the digger at him, he saw a rock bounce off Baby Bum's left temple. His eyes closed at the moment of impact and he was thrown off balance, causing him to miss Jim. The momentum of his charge carried him to the edge of the water on the opposite side of the skiff from where the dory was beached.

Before he could recover, Jim scrambled to the dory side of the skiff. He grabbed an oar and smashed it across Baby Bum's chest knocking him into the water.

Trying to claw his way out the oversized coat, dripping with water, weighed him down. His blood-streaked eyeballs protruded from their sockets. His twisted teeth snapped like a mad dog's.

Using the oar like a lance Jim jumped over the skiff and drove the end of it into Baby Bum's stomach dumping him into the water a second time.

"Jump in! Jump in, Jim!" Claudine screamed as she pelted Baby Bum with more rocks. "I've got the boat."

Jim turned and in three steps was aboard the dory. He drove the oar into the ground and gave it a mighty shove, propelling the boat and skiff out into the cove. Claudine pulled on her oars as hard as she could and in a moment they reached a safe distance from Baby Bum.

"I'll get you brats! As sure as my name is Baby Bum, I'll get you!" he screamed.

Jim stood up in the dory and yelled back at him, "If you had any brains, you'd get out of here. The police and everybody else in the village are looking for you."

"Is that so? Then why ain't they with ya now? They didn't believe you brats did they? Well, let me tell you something. Nobody takes what belongs to Baby Bum without suffering for it."

"We never took anything of yours," Jim argued.

"You took that boat," he screamed at them.

"This boat!"

"Yes, that boat. I found it adrift. That makes it mine."

"You are one sick person," Jim yelled across the water. "You steal our boat, and then you claim it's yours. Well, I'm going to tell you something. We figured it was you who had our boat and we thought you'd be waiting in ambush for us. You can see how much you scare us. We came and got it anyway. Only we had a little surprise for you. Well, if we see you around here again, we'll have an even bigger surprise for you."

Baby Bum glared at Jim. "Ya ain't foolin' me. Ya're plenty scared. Ya could have finished me off just now, but you ran off instead. If ya know what's good for ya, ya'll sleep with one eye open!"

A Stone Teepee

Chapter III

They rowed out of Indian Cove. "That's got to be the creepiest person I've ever seen in my life!" Claudine said.

"He sure is!" Jim agreed. "We've got to figure some way to protect ourselves from him. I thought sure he'd get out of these parts, but I guess he's made up his mind to get us."

"So what are we going to do?"

"We'll come up with something. But for now, we've got to come up with an explanation for not having any clams."

"Why don't we just tell the truth?" she asked. "Our boat went adrift. We don't have to say anything about Baby Bum."

They moored the two boats, removed the oars and clam digging gear, and walked home. Mrs. Collins and Mrs. Grant met them in the yard.

"Where have you two been?" Mrs. Collins demanded.

"The skiff went adrift in the fog," Jim said.

"And it took all day to find it?" Mrs. Grant asked.

"Gee, Mom! You can't see fifty yards out there," Claudine argued.

"They've most likely spent the day trying to figure out why crabs walk sideways or some other such nonsense!" Mrs. Collins said to Mrs. Grant.

"I wouldn't be surprised," Mrs. Grant replied. "In the future you two make sure you let us know when you're going to be late."

The next morning after breakfast, Jim met Claudine in the yard. He had a saw in his hand.

"What's that for?" Claudine asked.

"I'm going to cut a couple of maple poles for weapons. We'll learn to use them the way Robin Hood's men did."

"Terrific!" she said. "And we've got time to practice before we go clamming."

"Right! Now the way I see it, the most important trick we have to learn is how to keep the attacker from grabbing them away from us. Once the enemy gets a good grip on the staff, it would be as much of a weapon for him, as for us."

"Who's going to be first?" she asked.

"You are. You make fake swings at me, and I'll try to take it away from you. Be careful you don't really clobber me!"

After an hour of practice, they had gotten pretty good with the hard-maple staffs. "Good enough for now," Jim said. "We'll practice again when we get back from clamming and some more tomorrow morning."

"What about Baby Bum? What if he comes after us today?"

"There's no fog today, so I doubt if he'll show his

face. We'll keep away from the bog by picking a spot in the open so he can't surprise us or sneak up on us."

After loading their things into the boat, Claudine sat in the stern and Jim did the rowing. "Jim?" Claudine said with a note of confusion.

"What?"

"What's wrong with being inquisitive?"

"Nothing!"

"Then why does everybody think we're a pair of brats, always getting into trouble?"

"Baby Bum is the only one who has ever called us brats."

"Sure! But everybody thinks we're brats," she argued.

"Not really."

"They do, too."

"Well, I guess people do get annoyed at us," Jim agreed.

"Why?" Claudine insisted.

"It's what they call 'making waves', 'stirring muddy waters', and things like that. Grown-ups don't like being asked about things they don't understand or don't know anything about. They hate having their superstitions questioned. That's all there is to it. That's why they get upset with us."

"But it's our curiosity that makes you and me top students. We work hard. We don't waste our money on foolish things, and we've never given our parents any trouble. I just don't understand why they treat us like we're going to get into some kind of trouble all the time."

"'Curiosity killed the cat. That's their attitude. They don't seem to realize that if it wasn't for curiosity, we'd still be living in the stone age!" Jim replied.

"It must be the history of this place that's made the people the way they are." she added. "There's been all kinds of lawlessness and violence. I heard my grandfather tell that when he was a boy, there wasn't a week went by that somebody didn't get shanghaied from this village."

"I think you're right," he agreed. "Look at the Callahan place. A man's life wasn't worth two cents in that place. And the rum runners, they were something else! But did you ever notice it's when we start asking questions about the monument they really get annoyed with us? Even the constable used that as an excuse to ignore what we told him."

"I've noticed," she said. "It's like the other things have come and gone, but that stone teepee is still a threat to them."

"Ha! That's good! It does look like a stone teepee at that. Well, I'll tell you something, Claud. Baby Bum or no Baby Bum; before this summer is over I'm going into that monument."

"And I'm going with you," Claudine insisted.

"But your parents have forbidden you to step foot on that island."

"I'll worry about that when the time comes."

"It's okay with me," he agreed. "If you're game, so am I."

They arrived at their digging spot. Jim, followed by Claudine, took their clam diggers and slatted peck baskets from the boat. They looked for a good place to dig.

Jim found a spot with hundreds of little holes. Each hole had a diameter the size of a pencil. He bent over and began to dig. By pushing his digger into the surface to the right depth, and turning the muddy sand over, about half of the clams' bodies became exposed. Using both hands, he picked them from the ground and placed them in his basket. It took him a half-hour to fill both baskets. Not until they were filled could he straighten his back and give it a short rest.

With the baskets filled, he walked the short distance to the water and dipped them in and out several times to wash away the sand and mud. He then placed the clams in a wet burlap bag.

He returned to his original digging spot and repeated the process. By the end of the tide he and Claudine had spent about six hours stooped over pulling hard on their diggers.

When the tide finally covered the flats again they sat in the boat for a few minutes and gave their weary backs and aching muscles a chance to rest before beginning the long row home.

With the skiff loaded with clams, Jim had to row carefully. The weight of the load set the boat in the water so far that only a few inches of freeboard remained above the surface.

Once onshore they unloaded their clams and joined the other diggers waiting for the buyer. Claudine turned a basket upside down and sat on it. "In a way, I wish we didn't have to work, so we could give all our attention to getting out to the island," she said.

"You and me, both," Jim agreed.

"Here comes Mrs. Kenney," she said.

A pickup truck stopped in front of them. Mrs. Kenney was a big, burly woman married all of her life to the same dress without benefit of laundry. She measured the clams in an old, stretched-out bushel basket and rounded the top off until she couldn't put another clam on without it falling off.

Every time Jim and Claudine sold their clams to her they would become more furious about being cheated. Today, Jim couldn't hold back any longer. As she started to measure his he asked, "Why don't you put sideboards on that basket? Then maybe you can get two bushels for the price of one!"

Mrs. Kenney bolted upright. "If you don't like the way I do things, you can always sell to someone else."

"There's nobody else and you know it," Jim snapped.

She put her hands on her hips and glared at him. "Then you're kind of stuck with me, ain't you, sonny?"

Jim glared right back. "It kind of looks that way," he said angrily.

Claudine charged into the argument. "It's one thing to cheat kids, but these men have families to support. I think what you're doing is terrible. You should be ashamed, cheat ing poor people."

"You two brats had better shut up or I won't buy your clams anymore."

That gives me an idea!" Jim turned to Claudine. "Let's introduce her to Baby Bum. Just think what a beautiful couple they'd make!"

Claudine laughed. "For all we know, he's her husband!"

Their laughter irritated Mrs. Kenney. "Who's Baby Bum?" she asked.

"He's a friend of ours just like you're a friend of ours!" Jim answered.

"Wait a minute!" Claudine said. "You don't know Baby Bum?"

"Never heard of him. Sounds to me like someone you kids dreamed up."

They looked at each other with disbelief. "Then the tall man must have been his partner," Jim said.

"That's right!" Claudine agreed. "He's the one who must have sold the clams for both of them."

"What are you two babbling about?" Mrs. Kenney demanded in frustration.

"Have you bought clams from a tall, lanky man?" Jim asked.

"There are a lot of tall, lanky men around here. Times ain't so good that anybody's got extra fat on them."

Jim was tempted to tell her she managed to pile on a few pounds. "He'd be a stranger around here. My guess is you would have seen him near Indian Cove."

"Oh, him. What about him?"

"Well, do you know his name?"

"No, I don't. I just buy clams. I don't care about people's history."

"I don't think you care about people, period," Claudine said angrily.

"Now let's not start that again," Mrs. Kenney snapped. "If it wasn't for me, everybody here would be going hungry."

"Seems to me you're the one who just said people haven't got any extra fat on them around here," Claudine rebutted.

"You kids want to sell me these clams, or not? 'Cause if you do, you had better shut up. I've already wasted enough time here. One more word out of either of you, and you'll find yourselves stuck with 'em."

"May I ask a question?" Jim inquired politely.

"It better not be anything smart-alecky."

"You told us not to say another word, but if we don't, how will we answer your question?"

"What question?"

"Whether or not we want to sell you our clams."

"Oh, that. Well, do you, or don't you?" she demanded.

"You haven't said if he can answer your question yet," Claudine said coyly.

"Oh, my God! What have I done to deserve this? Yes, answer my question."

"Yes," said Jim.

"Yes, what?" Mrs. Kenney screamed.

"Yes, we're going to sell you our clams. If.."

"If, what?" she demanded, now clearly exasperated.

"If you use this new basket to measure them in," Jim insisted.

"Give it to me," she said. "Anything to get away from you two before you drive me crazy!"

They were pleased with themselves. They were cheated again, but at least it wasn't as much as in the past. As they walked home, Claudine screamed in frustration, "I can't stand being cheated by that woman!"

"Neither can I," Jim agreed. "There must be something we can do about it."

"We could try to find somebody else to sell to."

"If we had a car or something we could try some of the other villages."

"Why don't the men get together? They could hire a truck and go to Portland or even Boston."

"Nah, you know how everybody is around here," Jim said disappointedly. "They're all scared to try anything."

"Maybe we can show them how to do it," Claudine said.

"How?"

"I don't know right now," she answered. "But we'll think of something, you'll see."

"I think we've got enough problems for now, so let's get to practicing with our weapons. Let's get some burlap bags and string to put on the ends so we don't brain ourselves!"

"Good idea!" Claudine agreed. "Wait here. I'll be right back."

After about an hour of practice they both sat on the ground, exhausted. "You know we're getting pretty good," Claudine said.

"We sure are," Jim agreed. "The football helmets you brought were a good idea. This is really a lot of fun! Why don't we figure out a scoring system? We could turn this into a real exciting sport."

"Okay. Let's make it three points for a blow to the head; two, for a leg; and one, to the body."

"Why two for a leg and only one point for a body blow?"

"Because a good blow to the leg would put an opponent down, and then it would be easy to finish him off."

"You know? You're pretty smart for a girl," he said admiringly.

"Girls are every bit as smart as boys," she said, irked by his remark.

"I didn't mean it that way. What I meant was you're pretty smart about fighting and things like that. You have to admit most girls don't think much about giving a murderer a good beating," Jim argued.

"And boys don't think much about fighting murderers, either," she insisted.

"Okay, I lose. You sure got a good point there. Let's

get the padding off the end of these things. They won't do us much good like this if we need them in a hurry."

"Let's practice on the beach tomorrow morning," Claudine said. "I'm a little nervous about being where Baby Bum could sneak up on us."

"You're right," Jim agreed. "This isn't the wisest place for us to be right now."

"You know something? I hollered your name when Baby Bum attacked us at Indian Cove. Do you suppose he knows who we are and where we live?"

"I think we'd better plan on him knowing both of us."

"You don't think he'd be crazy enough to come right to our houses?" Claudine asked.

"He couldn't do anything that would surprise me. Put all kinds of glass junk on your bedroom windowsill. And put things that can get knocked over easily near your door and between your bed and door. Be sure to keep your staff handy all the time. And don't be afraid to scream, even if you just think he's snooping around."

"You going to do the same?" she asked.

"You'd better believe it! Okay, that's enough for today. We've got just about time enough to get to the Coast Guard Station before we have to be home."

In less than a half-hour they arrived at the station. They went inside and asked the seaman if they could see the chief. The seaman led them to a small office at the rear of the building and introduced them to the Chief Petty Officer in charge.

"What can I do for you?" the Chief asked pleasantly.

"We'd like some information about the monument on Stage Island," Jim said.

"I'm afraid I can't help you there," he replied.

"You can't?"

"No. I've tried to find out what that thing is all about, myself. But nobody seems to know anything about it. The Coast Guard didn't build it because we don't have any record of it anywhere."

Jim and Claudine looked at each other, disappointed. They thanked the Chief and walked home slowly.

A Gruesome Find

Chapter IV

A week and a half went by without any sign of Baby Bum. They were quite sure he had left the area. Nevertheless, they practiced with their staffs every day and took every precaution to protect themselves. As each day passed without incident they felt more secure.

On Monday morning of the third week in July, Jim suggested they go to Wooded Point to get a better view of the Monument.

"How are we going to do that?" Claudine asked.

"There's one tree on the point that stands half again higher than any of the others," he said. "It's an easy tree to climb. So we'll climb to the top and see what we can with these binoculars."

"I don't think that's going to be much help," she argued.

"It most likely won't be, but let's give it a try anyway."

"Okay," she agreed. "But I want to walk along the beach. We might as well stay out in the open as much as possible."

An older gentleman greeted them on their way to Wooded Point. "Well, how's Robin Hood and his lady this morning?"

"We're fine, sir," Jim replied.

"Aren't you going to try to beat each other's brains in with those clubs this morning?"

Claudine smiled at him. "No, sir, not this morning. We're going to Sherwood Forest to capture some of the King's men!"

"Oh, to be young again and full of imagination," the old man said chuckling to himself.

At the point they hesitated reluctant to enter the woods. There were so many trees the sky was nearly hidden from view. Even the sunlight found it difficult to penetrate the tangle of branches. The "forest" floor was covered with pine spills, forming a thick covering as soft as a mattress.

When Jim was younger he would spend hours in the tall tree. From the bottom all he could see was the forest as if the entire world was made up of trees and shade. Only two-thirds of the way up the whole world would explode into view.

On the left he would see a mile and a half of wide, sandy beach. In front of him would stand the string of islands that protected the beach from the violence of winter storms. And on his right would be the Atlantic Ocean.

He would watch the lobster boats and imagine himself at the helm of his own boat. Like Columbus, he would watch the sailing ships leave the harbor and sail out over the horizon. First their hulls disappeared over the horizon and eventually even the tops of their masts could not be seen. Jim remembered reading that it was this phenomenon that convinced Columbus the world was round.

It was the broad expanse of water that excited him the most. From his treetop perch he could actually detect the curve on the ocean's surface. Unlike the land where the open spaces were blocked off by fences, roads and buildings, the sea stretched all the way to England or South America and even India without anything obstructing the way.

He looked forward to climbing the tall tree again. At its base, Claudine caught Jim by the arm with her left hand. "What's that over there?" she asked.

Jim crouched down to get a better view. "Looks like a junk car."

"How'd a junk car get in here?"

"I don't know. Let's get a better look at it."

"Okay, let's go."

"Stay sharp," Jim warned. "I'm not too sure I like the looks of this."

"It's kind of spooky in here."

"Yeah, it is," Jim replied. "But it sure is peaceful. I could lay down on these pine spills and sleep for a week."

Claudine reached the abandoned car first and looked into it. "Hey! Somebody's been living in this thing! There's a bunk and shelves. And look at the way the camp stove and food are set up."

"That's pretty clever," Jim said. "Who'd ever think there was enough room in a junk car for all that stuff."

Claudine walked around to the other side. "Jim! Come here, quick!" she said with a hushed voice.

"What's the matter?"

"Look!" she replied, pointing to the ground.

"Uh oh!" Jim looked at the clam baskets and burlap bags. "This must be Bay Bums hideout!"

"We'd better get out of here, fast," she warned.

"Wait a minute. Maybe we can find something that will tell us who he really is or who the murdered man was."

"I think we should get out while the getting is good," she warned again.

"Oh, come on, Claud," Jim said impatiently. "You're going to give up now when we're this close?"

"I guess you're right," she agreed. "My curiosity would kill me and we'd just have to come back again some other time."

"Good. Let's see if we can spot anything through the windows."

"Look out!"

Her warning was too late. Baby Bum struck him from behind with his steel lunch box. The blow knocked him out and he dropped to the ground.

Baby Bum screamed with all the power of his lungs and lunged at Claudine. She swung one end of her staff with expert accuracy, knocking the lunch box out of his hand while at the same time jumping to one side. As he missed her she drove the other end of her staff against his back sending him sprawling to the ground.

Jim shook his aching head. He started to get back on his feet, then fell to the ground again.

Baby Bum bounced back. His only weapon was the murderous, four-pronged digger. He stood in a crouch facing Claudine. He looked fiercer than ever. He faked a charge from the left then again from the right. He thrusted forward a step and stopped. He circled Claudine, first one way then the other.

His movements were so quick that Claudine was getting dizzy. Everything about him was in motion. His wild, brown hair thrashed around on his head in every direction. His eyes were opened so wide it looked like his eyeballs could roll right out of his head. Then they closed into mean, little slits. His jaw vibrated like a mad dog's with spit running down his chin.

Baby Bum's huge coat puffed out all over his body looking like it was more eager than him to get Claudine. Even the oversized belt around his middle seemed angry. The loose end darted back and forth like the tongue of a snake.

She felt the effects of his gyrations. She knew if she didn't do something fast he would win. She changed her defensive stance and attacked. She faked a blow at the four shiny, steel blades instantly propelling the opposite end of her staff striking a hard blow to his forearm.

She jumped back a step and then charged forward bringing the raised end of her staff down toward Baby Bum's head. She missed and struck his left collarbone. He screamed more fiercely than ever, "I'm gonna drive these blades through both ya're eyes!"

He charged head-on and aimed his digger at Claudine's head. She ducked to one side and struck a blow to his ribs and another to his back. He went down, narrowly missing Jim. She charged quickly and struck him again.

Baby Bum planted his feet determined not to yield again. His face was red with rage. He concentrated on the lethal staff, but before he could make another attempt to strike her Jim had recovered sufficiently enough to join the fight.

There was no way he was going to face the two of them, so he turned and vanished among the trees. His shrieking voice came through the woods. "I'll cut off both yaw hands the next time. Both of them. Ya here me? I'm gonna git my friends and we're gonna cut off yaw hands and then cover ya with red ants!"

"You don't have any friends, Baby Bum," Jim hollered. "The next time we meet, we're going to break all your bones and then turn you over to the police. Just so you'll know we mean it, we're going to burn your place down."

"Ya burn my place, and I'll burn yaws," he warned.

"You're all washed up, Baby Bum. Watch! Here comes the pretty fire!" Jim dumped the fuel out of the camp stove and ignited it.

"Do you think that's wise?" Claudine asked. "It could set the whole woods on fire."

"That's the chance we're going to have to take. One thing's for sure, there won't be any Baby Bum in these woods by the time the fire department finishes putting this fire out. Come on! Let's get out of here!"

Baby Bum's voice now a thing of agony. "I'm gonna kill you brats!" he cried.

Claudine shuttered. "Ugh! Did you ever hear such a sound?" she asked.

Jim looked over his shoulder in the direction of the piercing voice. "Sounds like all the insanity in the world giving its last dying breath." As he spoke he felt goose pimples on his arms.

Jim stopped walking. He reached out and stopped Claudine who was a couple of steps behind him. "There's no way of knowing where he is now or where his voice is coming from in these woods. You keep an eye out behind us and to the right. I'll watch the front and to the left."

He was careful to avoid any tree big enough to hide Baby Bum. He moved slowly, looked for any signs of movement and listened intently for any sound that would tell him where Baby Bum was.

Suddenly a blue jay squawked a warning which startled a red squirrel. Jim and Claudine jumped in their tracks.

It took only a moment for their nerves to settle back to normal. They began to move toward the beach again. Shortly they arrived at the edge of the woods.

Jim stopped Claudine. He studied the trees which stood between them and the beach. He looked to the left and then to the right. "He could be hiding behind those rocks at the edge of the beach," he whispered. "We'll move through the rest of the trees just the way we've been doing. Then when we get to the rocks, we'll stop for a second, look things over, and if nothing happens, we'll run out on the ledge and jump out on the beach as far as we can. If he's behind the rocks, we'll have him trapped, and this time we're going to take him. Okay, are you ready?"

Claudine nodded in agreement then gave Jim a little push to get him moving. As they landed in the sand they spun around ready to fight.

Jim stood in a crouch with his staff held crosswise in front of him. Once he realized Baby Bum was not there his muscles began to loosen. He took one more careful look, raised his staff over his head and let himself fall over backwards into the soft sand.

"Oh, boy! Did you ever give him a thumping!" Jim

shouted in delight. "Wowee! I'll bet he won't forget you for the rest of his life! If Eve had been like you she would have stuffed the apple down that snake's throat instead of giving it to Adam!"

"I'm some glad you thought of this Robin Hood stunt," she said excitedly. "How's your head?"

"It hurts. He must have that lunch box full of rocks or something. I never saw so many stars in my life."

Claudine laughed. "Well, all I have to say is you're lucky he hit you on the head. Otherwise, you could've really gotten hurt."

"Ho, ho, ho! Maid Marion has a sense of humor," Jim mimicked.

"You'd better stick your head in the water and let me wash the blood off before we get home. I did all the fighting and you got all the bruises," she teased.

"Ouch! Go easy, will you?"

"I'm not hurting you," she insisted.

"With your sense of humor, I mean."

Moments later they heard the fire trucks. "Won't be long now. The firemen will be all through those woods," Jim said. "Baby Bum is going to get out of here now. There's no place left for him to hide."

"We still had better be mighty careful until we're sure he's gone," Claudine warned.

"That's for sure. hey! We'd better hustle. The tide's going down."

While Jim was eating lunch his mother noticed the injury on his head. She insisted on knowing how he had gotten hurt. He did his best to be evasive without lying outright.

"There's something very strange going on and I'm going to get to the bottom of it," Mrs. Collins said. "You take your sandwich with you. We're going next door. You and Claud are going to give us some answers."

"Oh, come on, Mom. You're making a mountain out of a molehill," Jim protested.

"Never mind the nonsense. You're coming with me,"

Mrs. Collins insisted.

Mrs. Collins told Mrs. Grant why she was there. "Have you noticed if Claud has been acting as strangely as Jim?" Mrs. Collins asked.

"They always have their heads in the clouds," Mrs. Grant said. "But lately, yes, Claud has been acting stranger than usual."

"Yes, well I thought so. Look at the bump on Jim's head," Mrs. Collins said. "Now you two children are going to sit here until you tell us what's going on."

"Well, Claud, what do you think?" Jim asked. "We don't have much choice, do we?"

"No, I guess we don't." As she looked at the mothers, Claudine said, "You're not going to believe us, but you're the ones who insist."

They told them the story. Mrs. Grant scolded them. "You should have told us immediately. If the constable wouldn't do anything we could've called the State Police."

"What for? They won't believe us either," Jim insisted.

"That's nonsense!" Mrs. Collins said. "You two have done a lot of things. God knows you have been in your share of mischief, but you have never lied to us. Now we're calling the State Police. Nobody is going anywhere until they get here."

By the time the trooper arrived and questioned Jim and Claudine it was too late to go clamming. The trooper told the mothers he was going to pick up the constable and they would spend the rest of the day searching the area. He didn't believe it would be difficult to find a character as unique as Baby Bum if he was still around.

Later that evening the trooper returned. "There is no way anybody fitting Baby Bum's description could be in the vicinity. We thoroughly searched the village and the shoreline.

"Baby Bum's description has been broadcast. If he's anywhere in the county, he will be picked up shortly."

The next day Claudine and Jim convinced their parents to let them go clamming. They promised to be very careful and to come home when the tide was over.

As they worked, Jim asked Claudine, "Do you think that trooper believed us yesterday?"

"I don't think so. At least he did something which is more than the constable did. I believe him, though. If he says Baby Bum isn't anywhere around then I don't think he is. Or at least he wasn't when they searched."

Jim stood up and stretched his back muscles. "The thing I've been trying to figure out is where could he go? If he tried to hitch a ride anywhere, he'd get caught. The only transportation he has is his rowboat. I don't think he'd be foolish enough to row out on the open sea to get to some other coastal village."

"Why not? He's crazy, isn't he?" she said.

"Crazy, yes, but not stupid."

"Mom said she wants us to dig on this side of the bog where they can keep an eye on us with the binoculars."

"Speaking of binoculars, we never did get to study the monument yesterday. What do you think of going to the airport? We could get a plane ride over the islands and really see what it's like. We could take a good look around for Baby Bum at the same time."

"Do you think our folks would let us go?"

"We can give it a try." Jim said. "We've never been in an airplane. It would be a real treat if we were going just for the ride."

The tide was all the way out. Jim finished filling his two peck baskets and walked down the channel to wash them. When he got there he saw something he had never seen before. "Claud! Claud! Come here, quick! Look!" he said as Claudine ran to him. "Did you ever see so many crabs in your life?"

"Oh, yuck! They give me the creeps! There must be thousands of them!"

"And then some. I wonder what they're after? It must

be a dead fish."

"No fish that big ever came in to the bay."

Get the oars out of the boat. After we scatter the crabs we'll be able to see what it is."

A mass of crabs of all sizes covered a mound more than six feet long, two feet wide and a foot high. Some of the crabs were as big as a hand and the smallest no bigger than a quarter. They were all moving and struggling to get to whatever it was their bodies covered.

They poked at the crabs with the oars and kept as far from them as they could. Their efforts only intensified the violent actions of the crabs.

"Can you see what it is?" Jim asked.

"No. Let's try to drive them off the end, instead of the middle."

After a few minutes Jim stopped. "That's not working either. I'm going to get the anchor and rope. We can try to hook it and pull it out of the water."

Jim was back in a minute with the anchor and line. He threw it so the point of the anchor would hook the thing. "I think I've got it," he said. "Give me a hand with it."

As they pulled on the rope they dragged the thing closer to the banking. Having reached the banking they pulled it out of the water. Claudine screamed and Jim vomited.

The "thing" was the body of the murdered man. Even out of the water hundreds of crabs attacked the corpse. One crab stared at Jim from a hole that had once held an eye.

Four Pecks To A Bushel

Chapter V

Claudine, like Jim, became very sick. The stench from the body was almost as bad as the sight of it. They could tell it was a human body, but beyond that there was nothing recognizable about it. After several minutes, Jim was able to ask Claudine is she felt all right.

"I'll never be all right again," she replied weakly.

Jim gulped a deep breath of air. "Me, neither," he agreed. "We have to get the police. Do you feel up to it?"

"Anything is better than staying here."

"That's for sure. But first we have to make sure they can find the body when they get here."

Claudine raised her hand in protest. "Well I'm not staying here with it!"

No, of course not." He reached into the boat and removed one of the wooden seats. "I'll use the anchor line and this seat. By tying one end of the rope to the body and the other to the seat, it'll form a buoy."

Jim took off his shirt and ripped it in half. He wrapped one-half around his face, covering his nose and mouth. He gave the other half to Claudine to do the same. "Now the stink won't be so bad." His voice was muffled, coming through the improvised face mask. "Take this oar and hold his leg up so I can tie the rope to it."

"Do I have to?" she protested.

"I'm afraid so."

Jim used a double half-hitch so he could attach the rope without having to touch the body. With that chore done they moved quickly away from it. "Now let's get the boat in the water and get out of here," Claudine suggested.

The boat they used on the flats had a flat bottom with a slight curve from the bow to the stern. This made is possible to slide across the mud flats with little effort.

Because the tide had gone out the rest of the way while they had been digging they had to move the boat about a hundred yards to get to the water.

Reaching the shore, they left their things in the boat and ran the rest of the way to the Grant house.

Mrs. Grant saw them coming. Jim realized by the look on her face she knew something was wrong.

Claudine ran to her mother's arms and began to sob. "What is it! What's the matter?" Mrs. Grant cried with alarm.

"We found the body," Jim explained. "It was horrible! We have to call the police."

Mrs. Grant helped Claudine into the house. "I'm okay now, Mom. You'd better call the police."

It only took ten minutes for the State Police cruiser to reach the Grant house. "I'll have to show you where it is," Jim told the trooper. "You'll need boots and something for a mask."

The trooper opened the trunk of the cruiser. "Thank you, Jim. The Coast Guard is going to meet us there. They're watching for us now."

"That's good, because I'm not going to stick around

while they recover the body."

Jim led the trooper down to the shore. By now the tide had turned and the bay was half flooded.

Once they were seated in the boat Jim began to row. You did a fine job, Jim, but I'm afraid I owe you an apology. I really didn't believe your story at first, but I guess I have to now."

"That's okay. At least you checked the place out and tried to find him. I want to thank you for that."

"I appreciate your thanks," he replied.

Jim nodded his head in acknowledgment then he shipped the oars. He turned in his seat and looked out over the water. "There it is," he said. "Just this side of the Coast Guard boat. See that board floating in the water? Well you'll find the body on the other end of the rope tied to it."

"Good! Now why don't you drop me off at the Coast Guard boat then you go home. I'll stop by and take your statement when I'm done here."

When the trooper returned to the Grant house he had Jim and Claudine repeat their story. After the questioning was finished he told them not to worry about Baby Bum. He said if he was anywhere near Stout Neck he would have him in custody within twenty-four hours.

The next day Jim convinced Claudine's parents and his own to let them take a bike ride to the airport. He told them it would help them get their minds off the horror of the previous day.

When they arrived at the airport they sought out Ralph Souler. They had watched him put on an air show at the county fair the year prior. They wanted to meet him ever since.

One of the stunts they saw him perform was shutting his engine off close to the ground then getting out of the plane and restarting the motor by hand while standing on the wing struts. Jim knew a man with that much courage was just the one to fly them over the monument.

As they walked with Ralph they told him they had never been up in a plane before. Jim asked him if he would fly them over the village.

He agreed and they were soon in the air. They were surprised at how small everything was. It appeared as though the world had suddenly been transformed into toys; cars, roads, trees and buildings were as small as the model village they saw at a Lionel Train show. The river and falls and even the large factory buildings made up a dream-like fantasy world that was much prettier than it appeared from the ground.

They were even more surprised at being able to see their village, nine miles away, after the plane had gained only a thousand feet of altitude. From the sky their village was unfamiliar to them. Jim looked at the landscape and had difficulty recognizing anything. Claudine jerked her head around from the window toward Jim. She beat on his arm with the back of her right hand. "There's my house! Isn't that something! It's no bigger than a deck of cards!"

Jim leaned close to her to get a better look. "Hey! There's mine!" he shouted. "Everything looks so small and nowhere near as crowded as it does from the ground. It's like things have shrunk and now there's room."

Jim asked Ralph if he could fly lower and along the shore. "I want to see if I can spot something."

Ralph agreed and banked the plane sharply to the left. The wing pointed straight down at the water. Jim and Claudine felt their bodies press hard into the seats.

Jim whispered into Claudine's ear to watch for any signs of Baby Bum. A few minutes had passed and he tapped her shoulder, "Nothing!" he said shrugging his shoulders in frustration.

He turned his attention to Ralph. "How about flying over the islands for us?" Ralph nodded his head in agreement.

They looked intently as the plane got closer to the monument. "Could you buzz by the monument for us?" Jim asked.

"Why do you want to go by that thing?" Ralph said with a disturbed look on his face.

"We've never gotten a good look at it," Jim explained.

"Too many gulls down there. If a bunch of gulls hit the plane it would be the end of all of us."

Jim hid his disappointment. "Okay. Can you just circle the island? We can see pretty good from here anyway."

Claudine tapped Jim on arm. "There!" she said pointing. "See the opening?"

"Yeah, I do," Jim answered. "Look at the seagulls! There's thousands of them!"

Claudine's voice became hushed. "And none on the other islands. That sure is strange."

"What's that!" Jim pointed to a spot on the mainland side of the island."

"Where?"

"Over there! I thought I could see a boat hidden under the bushes!"

Claudine leaned closer to the window. "I can't see anything."

"We're too far away now," Jim said. "Could you make another pass over that spot, Ralph?" he asked.

"I've got to get back now, kids. We've already been out five minutes more than what you paid for."

As the plane left the island behind they saw him slump into his seat like he was relieved to be getting away from that place.

The plane glided onto the runway. As the wheels touched the world returned to it's normal size. They got out of the plane, thanked Ralph and began the long bike ride home from the airport. "Did you notice how nervous he got flying near the monument?" Claudine asked.

"Did I! He was so tense he grew two inches!"

They rode on for another mile without a word. Jim thought about the monument and the way everybody reacted to it. And was that really a skiff he saw hidden among the bushes? If it was, how did it get there? Who did it belong to? And where was the owner? As his thoughts wandered he remembered an incident the winter before that could possibly be the connection between the monument and the river.

He pictured the huge snowdrifts that isolated the village from the city for over two weeks. He recalled how the people began to run out of food and the men organized themselves into rescue parties. One was to try with toboggans and the other was going to go up the river.

Claudine broke his train of thought when she pulled off the road for a drink of water at what was called the 'Half-Way Spring'. They sat next to the spring and rested. Jim drew lines on the ground with a stick. Finally, he looked up and began to express his thoughts. "Remember last winter when everybody was pleased when the men who tried to go up the river for supplies had to turn back because of the rough water?" Claudine frowned. " I've wondered about that. Shouldn't they have been disappointed?"

"Exactly!"

"Well, then, why weren't they?"

"Must've been because they were scared of the river, I guess."

"But why?" she insisted.

"I don't know why. That's something else we're going to ask Mr. Sidebottom."

Claudine became intent. "I wonder if there is any connection between their fear of the river and the monument."

"Yeah, that's exactly what I've been wondering!"

During the remainder of their trip they tried to understand the puzzle, but by the next day they had another problem to occupy them.

They came in from clamming and joined the other diggers waiting for Mrs. Kenney. "How long are you going to let that awful woman cheat you?" Claudine asked them.

The men looked up and one of them dared Jim and Claudine. "We don't see you kids doing much about it."

"It isn't up to us," Claudine rebutted. "You're the men. You should do something about it."

"What would you suggest, girl? another asked.

"I don't know," Claudine said thoughtfully. "Rent a truck or something and haul them to Portland or Boston. Maybe check somewhere else for an honest buyer."

One man got to his feet. "It's easy for ya kids to talk. Ya don't have families to support."

"It's not that easy for us, either," Jim argued. "We need the money just as much as anybody. Going to school and paying our own way is just as important to our families as it is to yours."

"That might be true," the first man said. "But eatin' regular and keepin' a roof over our heads is even more important as far as I'm concerned."

It was then that Mrs. Kenney showed up and started to cheat everybody impartially. Jim walked up to her determined she had cheated him for the last time. "Mrs. Kenney, if you want to buy my clams you will get four pecks to the bushel; not five, not six, four and no more!"

"Is that so?" she replied. "I'm the one who's got the money and I'm the one who's going to set the terms. You'll get like I say or you'll get nothing."

Jim scowled angrily. "Then it's going to be nothing. You've cheated me for the last time!"

"Ha! That's what I get for treating you better than the others. Brats! That's what you two are. Nothing but little trouble-making brats! Well, let me tell you something. You'll be back and you'll be begging. And you know what? When you do, I'll pay you exactly half of what I'm paying the others."

Claudine put her hands on her hips and leaned toward Mrs. Kenney until her face was only inches away. "Don't hold your breath!"

After everyone left, Jim and Claudine stood by the side of the road, wondering what to do with their clams. A car stopped in front of them. A woman passenger leaned her head out and asked if the clams were fresh.

"They certainly are, Ma'am. We just came in off the flats with them," Jim replied.

"How much are they for a peck?" the woman asked.

"Fifty cents, Ma'am," Claudine said before Jim had a chance to answer.

"Good!" the woman said. "I'll take a peck."

Jim could hardly contain himself until after she left. "Holy cow!" he shouted. "That's twice what we've been getting for them!"

"Let's set up a stand," Claudine suggested excitedly. "We'll run home, get into some good clothes and see what happens."

"Terrific!" We've got an old drop-leaf table in the barn we can use. Bring every box you can find. I'll make a sign."

Less than two hours later they had sold all of their clams. They made better than twice the money Mrs. Kenney would have paid them.

The news of their success spread through the village. Mrs. Tarbox called from the Neighborhood Store and told Mrs. Collins how everybody was excited. "It took a couple of kids to show us all that it's not necessary to be cheated by that woman!"

The following day they stopped digging an hour early. They rushed home, ate a quick lunch and changed their clothes.

Mrs. Collins had the stand ready for them when they got there. By the time the other diggers arrived, their clams were nearly all sold. By the time Mrs. Kenney showed up they had already started selling the other digger's clams.

The diggers told her if she wanted to treat them fairly they would sell to her, otherwise, they would sell what they could at the side of the road and dump the rest in the bay. Mrs. Kenney got in her truck and drove away without saying a word.

Another successful day had passed. As Jim and Claudine were congratulating each other Claudine asked, "Have you noticed the difference in the villagers?"

"Difference! I guess there's a difference! For the first time people around here seem to have something to be happy about."

"Now all we have to do is solve the mystery of the monument," she said. "And things might get back to normal around here."

"Not until we find out what happened to Baby Bum," Jim argued. "As far as the two of us are concerned, we're not going to be able to breathe easy until he is caught."

"Isn't that the truth. I wonder how come they haven't found him yet?"

Jim shrugged his shoulders. "Could be all kinds of reasons, I guess."

"I suppose. Well, let's go visit Mr. Sidebottom."

"It's kind of late for that, don't you think?" he argued.

"It isn't that late," she said. "Besides we don't have to start early tomorrow."

They told their parents they'd be gone for an hour or two. It took them about ten minutes to reach Mr. Sidebottom's house. Despite the short distance going to his house was like entering another world. There were no other houses near his and his driveway was white with crushed clam shells. In the dark it looked like a huge white fish being swallowed by the jawbones of the whale that formed the entrance and that was the only way into the house.

Claudine and Jim stood at the foot of the driveway. "Do you suppose he's gone to bed?" she said hoping for an excuse to keep from having to approach any closer.

"Maybe," Jim said, thinking he should take advantage of her excuse.

"Well?"

"Well, what?"

"Are we going in?" she asked.

"Let's not and say we did."

"Don't be funny," she said. "I'm willing if you are."

"Oh, my spirit is plenty willing, but my flesh won't move," he said nervously. "Well," he looked at Claudine and took in a big breath, "we're here, so let's go."

One Too Many Questions

Chapter VI

Claudine looked at Jim and said coyly, "You go first."

"What do you mean, I go first!"

"You're the boy."

"What's that got to do with anything?"

"Boys should go first in situations like this."

"Oh, no! It's ladies before gentlemen."

"Not this time."

"Are you taking advantage of me because you're a girl?"

"Yup. I'm also smarter than you. Men like to show how big and brave they are, so I'm going to be real nice and let you go first."

"Gee, thanks! I always knew you were a true friend."

"You're welcome," she said sweetly. "Now get going. I'm right behind you. I won't let anything happen to you!"

"Oh great! Having you protect me makes me feel a lot better!"

"I thought it would."

Jim stopped smiling. "Look, let's come right out and ask about the monument. Let's see if we can move the conversation in that direction. That is, if we even get into the place."

Suddenly Jim stopped and Claudine bumped into him. "Oh!" he gasped.

"What is it!" she said startled.

"I think I have a nail in my shoe," he said laughing.

"Jim Collins, you do that again and I'll give you a good kick in the shins. Now come on. We don't want to be here all night."

"Are you scared?"

"Of course, I'm scared. Doesn't this place give you the creeps?"

They finally reached the door and Jim just stood there reluctant to knock.

"Well, go ahead and knock," Claudine whispered.

As he continued to hesitate Claudine reached from behind him and rapped soundly on the door. Jim spun around with surprise. She looked at him and shrugged her shoulders. "It's sink or swim!" she said.

A voice from inside invited them in. Jim opened the door and stepped inside followed by Claudine. One look at Mr. Sidebottom calmed the fears the strange place had given them. He looked as gentle as his home looked fierce.

The inside of the house was as crooked as the outside. Even the furniture was lopsided. Mr. Sidebottom sat at a titled table and an uneven chair smoking a white, clay pipe. He looked like Santa Claus complete with hair and beard, pink cheeks and bright blue eyes. The only difference being his rolled down hip boots and gray, checkered shirt. "Well, now. To what do I owe the pleasure of this visit by the village heroes?"

"We're curious about something," Jim said.

"Curious!" Mr. Sidebottom chuckled. "You two have

enough curiosity for a hundred people!"

Claudine moved a little closer to the edge of her seat. "We just don't like unanswered questions. And we love to hear stories about this place. You've been here longer than anybody and I'll bet you know more about this village than everybody put together."

"I've been here for a long time, that's for sure. What would you like to know?"

"Tell us about the Callahan place," Jim asked.

"You sure you want to hear about it?"

"Sure! We both do."

"The story of the Callahan place has to start with Callahan himself," Mr. Sidebottom began. "It seems he had business in Portsmouth, England. He traveled all the way from Dublin, Ireland, on foot. Those were the days of sailin' ships and it was always hard to get crews. Well, Callahan was a stranger in Portsmouth and a long way from home. He stopped at a waterfront pub for a glass of ale. While he was there he was knocked unconscious and put aboard a British merchantman.

The British ship eventually landed in Boston. There he jumped ship and took a berth on an American vessel that sailed the coast of New England.

In those days there were no railroads, so cargo was hauled from one coastal town to the next by a large fleet of small sailin' ships.

When his boat landed here he jumped ship again and got himself work onshore."

Mr. Sidebottom took a large wooden match, scratched it on the bottom of his chair and relit his pipe. He took a big puff and continued to talk. "He was feelin' mighty mean over what happened to him and was bound he was goin' to get even with the world.

After awhile he built his inn for sailors. It was a bad place right from the beginnin'. Nobody with any sense would go near it. Any man who got drunk in there woke up with his money gone or aboard a ship if he didn't already have a crew.

One day a gypsy went in to Callahan's lookin' for work. Callahan gave him work. Not the kind the gypsy was lookin' for, though. He, too, ended up aboard a strange ship.

What Callahan didn't know was that the gypsy's family was camped right outside his place waitin' for their man to return. By the followin' night the gypsy woman had gone inside several times demandin' to know where her man was.

Well, Callahan got very mad after awhile. He sent a couple of toughs outside and they burnt the family's wagon. The woman and children cried, begging them to spare their home. The hardhearted men just laughed.

The woman and her children sat on the ground and cried. The man of the home was gone and all they owned lay before them in ashes. She took her two children inside the inn. Before the startled eyes of the people there she killed them, both. Then she cursed Callahan and his inn and then killed herself.

Within a month Callahan was put into an insane asylum. The last three weeks he had lived in his inn all by himself. Nobody would go near the place anymore, so horrible were the goings-on caused by the ghost of the gypsy woman and her two dead children."

Claudine choked. "That's horrible!"

"Is that true?" Jim asked.

"True, or not, there ain't been a soul who's stayed in that buildin' from that day to this!"

Claudine was wide-eyed. She looked at Mr. Sidebottom intently. "Mr. Sidebottom? Why is everybody around here scared of their own shadows?"

"'Cause they've always had plenty to be feared of. This village was born amidst violence and superstition.

"When folks began settlin' around here they were careful. They didn't want any trouble with the Indians. They're spected their customs and any land they took, they paid for; not with trinkets, but with things of real value like knives, axes and farmin' tools.

The Indians here and about were not savages like a

lot of people think. They farmed and fished and had laws and government just like we do today.

Around here they belonged to the Algonquian Federation. Their land went from the Mississippi to the Atlantic and from the Carolinas to Canada.

The head man was The Great Sachem (saw'-kim) or Basheba. His job was to administer the laws like our President does. Under him was a council that had the same job as our Congress.

Each tribe was headed by a sachem." He put down his pipe and his eyes became brighter than before. "And here's an interesting part. Around here, the sachem was called 'Squaw Sachem'! That's right! A woman was head of the local tribe!

Now even though the local settlers were very careful to keep good relations with the Indians at times there were strangers comin' up the river to trade. One day Squaw Sachem was crossin' the river in a canoe. She had her baby with her.

The men on a sailin' ship comin' up the river wondered if an Indian baby, like a wild animal, could swim from birth. They took Squaw Sachem's baby and threw it into the river. Of course, the baby drowned.

What she did next was to curse the river. She told the sailors that three white men would drown every year on the river forevermore! Well, you know? For as long as anyone can remember, three white men have drowned in the Saco River every year!

Shortly after that the Indian wars broke out. About the only people to survive were those who took refuge in the stone fort that used to be on Fort Hill. 'Fort Mary' it was called."

Claudine was sitting on the very edge of her chair. "That must have been the reason people were so nervous last winter when the men tried going up the river for food."

"That's about the size of it," Mr. Sidebottom agreed. "The river is cursed and they're scared of it."

Jim hung onto every word he was saying. "What did happen to the fort on Fort Hill and how did one end up on Wooded Point?"

"Now there's about the easiest question you've asked tonight. About the time I was a young man Fort Mary had pretty much fallen apart. Some city fella with more money than brains tore down what was left of it. Then usin' the stone he salvaged he built himself a bathhouse on the shape of a small fort of Wooded Point."

Claudine was shocked. "You've got to be kidding!"

"Nope. That's just what he did."

"He didn't have much sense of history," Jim suggested.

"Nor the folks who let him do it," Mr. Sidebottom agreed. "I think the reason folks around here don't show interest in the history of this place is they'd like all these things to disappear from memory, so they could sleep better at night."

He shifted his weight in his chair and began to clean his pipe. "Look at the way they let the old Jordan Mansion go to pot. That house set on the very spot where Richard Vines spent the winter of 1616. Him and his crew were the first white men to spend the winter in what was to become the United States of America! It was his report to Sir Fernando Gorges of the Plymouth Company that brought about the settlin' of Plymouth by the Pilgrims.

Vines and his crew built the fireplace in their cabin from stones they picked up on White Beach and thatched the roof with straw they collected from the very bog where you two saw the murder take place!

Now this all took place on the shore of Indian Cove just across from Fort Hill. Like I said, the Jordan Mansion was built on the very same spot about 1700. At the time of the Revolutionary War Captain James P. Hill lived in the Jordan Mansion. He was a member of the Committee of Safety. Many of the most important patriots of the American Revolution met and planned strategy there."

"Wow! That has to be one of the most historical places in this country!" Jim said excitedly.

At the same instant Claudine said, "That's incredible! How on earth did you ever learn all of this stuff?"

"I got papers and things. Been handed down to me from my kin," Mr. Sidebottom explained.

Claudine almost fell off her chair. "Do you still have them."

"I sure do!"

"Could we see them?" Jim asked wide-eyed.

"I guess so. If you promise to be real careful with them."

"Oh, we will! We promise! We'll be real careful!" they guaranteed eagerly.

Mr. Sidebottom opened a large steel box. From inside he removed a smaller box. "The first thing I'm goin' to show you is a letter from a soldier to his mother. The soldier was a great uncle of mine and the letter was written on the eve of the Battle of Bunker Hill. I'm goin' to lay it on the table so you can see it."

They stood on either side of Mr. Sidebottom. They bent over the letter for a better view. Each page had been placed between two sheets of glass. Wax sealed the edges so that no air could get to the old paper.

The soldier told how he was writing the letter by the light of his campfire. He described the scene of the encampment and how they expected a major battle soon.

Jim looked up from the letter to Mr. Sidebottom. He spoke with a hushed voice like he would if he were in a church. "I can almost feel his presence," Jim said. "It's like I was looking over his shoulder while he was writing this. He describes the scene so well. I can see the hill and campfires in my mind."

The feelings of reverence were so intense for Claudine she spoke with a near whisper. "The words are so formal and yet you can feel the love he had for his mother. It's really amazing, Mr. Sidebottom. I would have never believed looking at a piece of paper would give me the greatest thrill of my life!"

Mr. Sidebottom pointed to the words the soldier had written. "See how beautiful the writin' is? Every letter is made perfect and the way he signed the letter, 'Your obedient servant and loving son'. You don't see fine manners like that anymore."

"It's really a beautiful letter," Claudine said. "It gives me goose bumps just looking at it."

"That's good, 'cause that's the last letter he ever wrote. He was killed the very next day."

"Oh!" she gasped.

Mr. Sidebottom very carefully put the letter to one side. Then he reached into the big, steel box and took out old newspaper clippings and magazine articles telling of shipwrecks and other important events of the times.

"Now here's a long letter from my great grandfather to his brother that tells the story of the Jordan Mansion and Captain Hill who I've already mentioned. The Jordan Mansion was a garrison house with a high wall around it. It had watch towers on all four corners. Actually, it was the first fort around here. Built even before Fort Mary!"

"If I live a hundred years, I don't think I'll ever have an experience to match this one," Jim said enthusiastically. "These documents are sensational!"

"Do you have anything that tells about the monument?" Claudine asked.

Mr. Sidebottom jerked his head upright. His eyes opened wide. "No!" he said sharply. "Nobody knows anythin' for sure about that place."

"But there must be a record of who built it and why," Jim insisted.

"Don't know anythin' about that," he snapped.

"Do you know if there's a plaque on it or any kind of identification?" Claudine asked.

"Nope, don't know. Ain't never been out there and if you've got any sense you'll keep away from there, too."

"But why?" Jim persisted.

" 'Cause it's an evil place," the old man argued. "I'm sure no more superstitious than the next man. All I know is that people have died out there for no good reason I could ever figure out. That monument never interfered with my life and I never felt I should interfere with it."

"It does sound bad at that," Jim said cautiously hoping not to antagonize Mr. Sidebottom. He wanted him to keep talking about the monument. "Could you tell us about some of the people who have died out there?"

"Well, I suppose I could. I don't like to talk about it, but I'll tell you about one time when folks figure several men died there."

Jim and Claudine returned to their seats. "There was a three-master haulin' coal. They had been fightin' a Nor'easter. Before they could make it into the harbor she went down.

None of the crew was ever found. That's not too surprising because when a ship goes down in a violent storm the crew doesn't have much of a chance.

The surprisin' thing was two of her lifeboats were seen on the shore of Stage Island not too far from the monument. After the storm a vessel stood off from the island. Lookouts were in the riggin', but they couldn't see anyone. Finally they fired muskets. Still there was no sign of life. After standin' most of the day they left."

"Didn't anybody go ashore to look for survivors?" Jim asked.

"They didn't figure there was sense riskin' good men to go find dead ones."

"Then nobody really knows."

"Nope. And there ain't anybody with good sense who's goin' to try to find out."

"Is that the only incident?"

"I said I'd tell you about one and that's all I'm goin' to tell you. There's been plenty of folks disappeared through the years around that cursed island and nobody has ever been able to give proper explanation."

"But no one ever went on the island to check for survivors."

"If anyone had been alive they could have shown
themselves and been rescued. They never did," he argued.
"Now, it's gettin' past my bedtime, so you two run along.
Your folks are goin' to be worryin' about you."

"Holy mackerel! Look at the time! Where did the
evening go?" Jim stood up to leave.

Claudine shook Mr. Sidebottom's by the hand. "Thank
you very much. I never had such an interesting evening. I'm
going to find history a lot more fascinating from now on."

"You're welcome, Claudine. Now don't you two be
strangers. An old man likes a little company once in awhile."

"Thank you, sir." Jim shook his hand. "You can count
on us coming again. Maybe you can teach us some of the
fine points of cribbage some evening."

"That's be fine. And don't you two get any foolish
ideas about goin' out to that island. You'd best leave well
enough alone. You don't bother it and it won't bother you."

"Yes, sir. And thanks again. It's been a real pleasure
visiting with you." They started down the driveway heading
for home. "What do you think?" Jim said.

"That's what I'm doing. Thinking."

"Well?" he persisted.

"Well, what? I don't know. How can we be so sure
there's nothing to all this stuff? Everybody in the world can't
be crazy."

"You're right," he agreed. "Everybody in the world
is not crazy, but just about everybody is superstitious. Let
something happen they don't understand and one way or another they're going to explain it. The easiest way for them is
to blame spooks. Why can't they just say they don't know?"

"Maybe, yes. Maybe, no. But who is going to guarantee when we go out there we'll come back!"

Off To A Bad Start

Chapter VII

Jim and Claudine kept their families up half the night telling them about the things they had seen at Mr. Sidebottom's.

For most of the following day their excitement caused them to keep up a constant chatter. It was the middle of the afternoon before they finally settled down. They were too busy at the stand to think of anything else but the customers. Word had spread that they sold the best and freshest clams anywhere. Each day they sold all of their own clams, plus those the other village men dug.

Claudine made a deal with the other diggers. She and Jim would take their clams and sell them at twice the wholesale value. They charged the diggers twenty cents on the dollar for running the stand, for shrinkage and overhead. Because Jim gave the diggers an honest measure they now earned twice as much money as before. Mrs. Collins and Mrs. Grant helped with the stand when Jim and Claudine couldn't be there.

As it got on toward suppertime Mrs. Kenney drove up to the stand. "How are you children doing?" she asked pleasantly.

"We children are doing fine," Claudine answered, annoyed by Mrs. Kenney's artificial sweetness.

Mrs. Kenney ignored Claudine and turned to Jim. "Business has been good I take it."

Jim was as irritated by her presence as Claudine. "And it's going to get a whole lot better."

"Did you have much trouble getting a license?"

"License? What license?"

"You don't mean to say you don't have a license?"

"No, we don't have a license," Claudine replied. "We're not driving a car; we're selling clams. So what do we need a license for?"

"Oh, you poor dears," Mrs. Kenney laughed gleefully. "You're running a store in which you are selling a perishable product. That's why you need a license."

"The only clams we sell are the ones that are dug on the same day we sell them, so they're not about to perish on us," Jim argued.

Claudine, now furious, "Look, Mrs. Kenney, you can stop putting on airs for us! All we want is for you to leave us alone."

"I'm just trying to be helpful, dear. I wouldn't want to see you nice, little brats end up in jail because of your ignorance of the law. Just remember when you get yourselves in trouble I was the one who told you so." Appearing satisfied that she had gotten the upper hand she drove off.

"Nice, old crow isn't she?" Claudine said angrily.

"I still think we should introduce her to Baby Bum if we ever get the chance."

"No thanks! Can you imagine their having a bunch of kids! I can see it now; a whole bunch of Baby Bums running around laying claim to the whole village, ocean, islands, the sky and anything else they could think of."

"That would be a disaster wouldn't it?" Jim said

laughing. "Well, we'd better find out about this license thing before we have a disaster of our own."

"Do you suppose what she said is true?"

"It must be. I'm sure she didn't make a point of stopping because she missed seeing us. She's most likely on the phone right now to whoever has charge of such things."

"So, what do we do about it?" Claudine asked. "We're going to turn it over to higher management. Our parents. Then you and I can concentrate on making another important decision."

"What decision?"

"Last night you wanted to know who would guarantee we'd make it back from the monument. The way I see it we have to make the decision to do it first. If we decide we will then we have to give it careful thought and plan it so we have everything in our favor. In other words, we're the ones who will guarantee our safe return."

"I thought we'd already decided about going," she argued.

"We did, but you didn't sound so sure of yourself last night."

"I'm sure," she said. "It's just I'm a little nervous about it."

"Well, so am I. It isn't exactly like going to the store for a quart of milk!"

"Okay, so what we have to figure out is how to get there and back."

"Right," he agreed. "I've been thinking about it and the way I see it we've got several problems. First, we have to have a proper boat for the trip. Then we have to consider the weather, the ocean the birds on the island, superstition and our own fears. Let's both think about it until tomorrow then we can put our ideas together and make a plan."

"Sounds okay to me. Let's clean up here. We've got to get home and tell our parents about Mrs. Kenney."

That night the two families met to discuss the problem. Mrs. Collins was delegated to call the county clerk in the morning to find out what was required for them to operate the stand.

Jim and Claudine were happy to be able to dump a problem onto someone else for a change. It was now the beginning of August and they were becoming anxious that the summer would be gone before they could get out to the monument.

If they missed their chance this summer they knew they would have to wait until the following year and they just couldn't wait that long.

The next day, while clamming, Jim suggested the biggest problem with making the trip were the superstitions and fear. Claudine agreed.

"First of all fear comes from superstition," Jim said.

"Not necessarily. Our fear of Baby Bum has nothing to do with superstition."

"True, but I'm talking about the monument. I think any fear we have about this trip is because of our own superstitions. Get rid of superstition and we get rid of fear."

"Easier said than done," Claudine argued. "The whole world is superstitious. Some people more than others, but we're all superstitious to a degree."

"Agreed, so how valid are superstitions? Is there any reason to justify them?"

"Plenty of reasons, I think. Superstition is everybody's answer to the unknown. People have to have answers. When they can't find a natural answer they create a supernatural one.

"When you get right down to it," she continued, "that's what we're all about. You and I insist on finding our own answers. Just because someone tells us something is so we don't accept it at face value. We'll keep right on digging until we're satisfied. In a way, that's a flaw in our characters. That's one of the reasons people get irritated with you and me. They can tell we don't accept what they say just because they say it. Personally, I think it's a good fault!"

"So do I," Jim agreed. "But how are we to explain what happened to Callahan? The man did go crazy within a few weeks after the gypsy woman cursed the place."

"Well, just think of the horror of the whole thing." Claudine stopped working so as to put more emphasis on what she was saying. "There was Callahan and a bunch of rough-type sailors. They shanghaied a man not knowing his family was nearby waiting for him. The woman went into the inn many times insisting to know what happened to her husband. They couldn't admit what they had done, so they burned her wagon which was her home. Her husband was gone. There was nothing left for her.

She goes into the inn with her children and killed them right in front of him, cursed the place and then committed suicide.

I think that would be enough to cause anyone to have nightmares. Even a man like Callahan. Especially when they were all superstitious to begin with.

From then on every sound, every creek of a board or squeak of a door convinced them that ghosts were present."

Jim nodded in agreement. "So, actually it's our imagination that gives proof a superstition is true."

"I think so. Now all we have to do is convince ourselves of that."

"Yeah!" Jim became very thoughtful. "I know what you mean. It's one thing to say it, but it's something else to really believe it. I guess we'll have to face up to it when the time comes, but for now let's figure out what we need.

I think we should use the dory," Jim continued. "We'll rig the sail on her and keep both sets of oars on board. We'll need extra rope, a first-aid kit, some sandwiches and water. Can you think of anything else?"

"Our staffs," she said.

"That goes without saying. We should have a couple of practice sessions before we go. Baby Bum still hasn't been caught, you know."

"He hasn't been seen either. I doubt if he's within a thousand miles of here."

"Even so, we'd better not plan on it," Jim cautioned.

"Oh, Jim, we'd better take a couple of life jackets along, too."

"Oh yeah. That's one thing we don't want to forget."

"So it's settled then. When do we go?" she asked.

"In a couple days. The tide will be just right. We'll be done work by noontime, so it'll give us at least seven hours to get out to the island and back. We'll ask to have the afternoon off to go sailing and our mothers can run the stand."

That evening and the next two days they used all of their spare time to get things ready. The mast had to be installed, the hull of the dory had to be scraped and cleaned and supplies prepared.

The morning of the trip Claudine greeted Jim with a big yawn. "I didn't sleep too good last night. I couldn't get my mind off our trip."

Her yawn got Jim started on one of his own. After a moment he shook it off. "Neither did I. The excitement was a little too much for me."

They got aboard the skiff and headed for their favorite spot to dig clams. As the day progressed they kept looking toward the water. The turning tide would be their signal that the beginning of their trip was near.

Once the water started to cover the flats that was their cue to load their clams into the boat. They returned home as quickly as they could, delivered the clams to the stand, had a quick lunch and loaded the dory.

Jim cast off from shore. Claudine raised the sail while Jim took the tiller. "We're on our way!" Jim shouted on the wind.

It was a sunny day with a brisk wind. The dory moved up the bay at a good speed toward the channel leading them to the ocean.

The swift current in the channel slowed their progress

to a crawl in spite of the good breeze. Jim moved the tiller slightly bringing the dory closer to the shore of the channel. This put her in the current's eddy moving her more quickly than on the open bay.

They were free of the channel within minutes and sailing over the big, bright, blue sea. They saw their destination near the horizon. The swells got larger as they moved away from the mainland giving the dory a rollercoaster effect.

"We'll have to land on the opposite side of the island from the monument," Jim said. "There's no place to beach a boat anywhere else."

"Why don't we circle the island and make sure," Claudine suggested. "I would rather land as close to it as possible."

"We can do that, but I don't remember seeing anything from the plane but the beach on the mainland said."

"No? I remember seeing a beach on the same side as the monument."

"But that's near a reef," Jim argued. "We could end up wrecking the boat."

"Well, the least we can do is check it out, right?"

"Sure, but I still think it will be too dangerous."

Claudine looked at him surprised at herself. "Will you look at us. We're not even halfway there and we're getting jumpy already."

"You're right," Jim apologized. "We'd better be careful or we'll blow it before we even get there."

Just then a large porpoise broke water a few feet from them. His quick intake of air made a sound like a pair of cupped hands being slapped together. Its sudden appearance caused them both to jump. As their nerves settled down they had a good laugh at each other.

"Maybe we should have brought our fish lines with us," Claudine joked.

"You don't catch fish when porpoises are playing games."

"That's true. At least having a porpoise around is a

good sign. Anyway, that's what sailors say."

"That's a superstition," Jim frowned.

"Maybe, but they do push drowned bodies to shore."

"You call that good luck! Having your dead body pushed ashore? Besides I never knew anyone who actually saw it happen."

"I didn't say good luck. I said it was a good sign."

"Good luck or good sign. What's the difference? It's superstition no matter how you look at it."

"So now you don't even believe in luck?"

"No, I don't," he agreed. "There's no such thing as luck, good or bad. There's chance, but not luck. If you buy a raffle ticket you have a chance to win. Luck has nothing to do with it. As far as I'm concerned believing in luck is no different than believing in superstition."

"Maybe you're right," she conceded. "Personally, I think we're lucky to live where we do with fresh air, the beach and the ocean."

"But that's not luck," he said impatiently. "That's chance. We happened to be born here instead of some place else."

"I suppose," she agreed. She looked away from Jim and studied the water. She had grown tired of the discussion. "The island sure looks big from here. It shouldn't be long now."

"Nope, just a little while longer will put us face to face with our moment of truth."

Claudine stiffened in her seat. "Holy cow! Quick! Put your life jacket on!"

A huge swell, about a hundred yards away, was rolling straight at them. It got higher as it came closer to their boat. At fifty yards the top began to lead the bottom in its race toward Jim and Claudine.

"It's going to break!" Jim screamed. "Hold on with all your might!"

Ten yards from them an explosion of white water crashed down from the top of the mountain of water. The solid wall of ocean upended the dory while at the same instant engulfing them.

Jim felt the water push in on him. It crowded into his eyes, nose and ears. It pressed hard into his body forcing his stomach muscles toward his spine.

The salt water burned his eyes as he tried to see the surface. He pushed water behind him with all his strength. With his breath about gone his head bobbed out of the water into the fresh air. All was peaceful on the surface. Too peaceful. Frantically he looked around for Claudine. "Claud! Claud, where are you?" he screamed.

"Over here! I'm over here! The dory is between us."

Jim swam to the boat where he could see her. "Thank God you're okay! Are you hurt?"

"I don't think so. Boy, we have got a job ahead of us!"

"That's for sure!" he agreed. "The mast is broken, but everything else looks okay. The oars! Where are the oars!"

They twisted around in the water. "Over there." Claudine pointed.

"I see one! I'll look near it for the others. You see what you can find on the other side."

They swam in a large circle around the swamped boat. Eventually they found all of the oars. The effort exhausted them. They clung to the overturned hull for several minutes to get their strength back.

Jim studied the situation. "If we're to have a chance of getting this boat right side up we're going to have to release the sail and mast. I'm going to get under her to release the mast stays, so watch out for me." Jim removed his life jacket.

"Let's tie the boom line around your waist, first. Just in case," Claudine suggested.

"Okay. When I dive, count to thirty. If I'm not up when you finish start to pull in the line."

Who Got The Blame?

Chapter VIII

It took several tries, but Jim finally got the mast and sail free from the dory.

He went underwater again. This time he came up inside the overturned boat. A large pocket of air was trapped between the bottom of the boat and the water. The air had to be released before the boat could be uprighted. He reached up and removed the large wooden plug from the boat's bottom. Immediately the air escaped causing the dory to settle further into the water eliminating the air space.

With the trapped air released Jim returned to the surface. They reached across the dory's bottom, planting their feet on the boat's side. By leaning backward as far as they could the boat rolled over and became upright.

Claudine reached inside and replaced the plug. While still in the ocean they began to splash water out of the dory with the oars. Once they bailed enough of it out of the boat they got in. From inside, they removed the rest of it. They rolled up the sail and rigging and began to row toward the mainland.

Jim pulled on the oars. "That was too close for comfort," he said.

"You got that right," she agreed. "But where did that breaker come from?"

"I don't know," Jim said looking puzzled. "Maybe it's like Lobster Rock. I've heard the fishermen say that a month can go by without seeing a breaker then all of a sudden three of them, ten to twenty feet high, will sweep the place clean."

"Sure, I can understand that," she said. "Lobster Rock is a ledge and you can always expect breakers in shallow water."

"You still can see breakers in deep water," Jim argued.

"In a storm you can, but not on a perfect day like this. Besides I've never heard anyone mention seeing breakers where we got swamped."

"So? What are you trying to say?"

"Nothing. It's strange, that's all."

"There you go," Jim said impatiently. "We get hit by a breaker and you're all set to start a legend of your own. I suppose you think some spook kicked it up to keep us from the island, huh?"

"I didn't say anything of the kind, smarty. I would just like to hear you give a reasonable explanation."

"Nature," Jim snapped at her. "Just plain, old Mother Nature. That's why we wear life jackets. Nature is always doing unpredictable things."

"That's it, huh? You're absolutely sure that's all there is to it?" she demanded angrily.

"Oh, come on, Claud. Let's not fight over it. I know I don't have all the answers, but I'm not going to spook myself either."

"Huh. And of course the next time you sail through

that area you're going to be as calm as the early morning sea," she teased.

"No, not really. I'll be on alert for another one."

"Yeah, I'll bet," she argued. "Of course there won't be any thought in your mind that maybe, just maybe, something we know nothing about might be waiting to hit us with another blow."

"Don't be silly. Don't breakers always come in three's?"

"Most of the time," he agreed.

"All of the time not just some of the time! Now you tell me why there was only one breaker that hit us." she challenged.

"I don't know, Claud," he shouted in frustration. "You want me to admit that I'm shook up by that wave? Is that what you want?"

"Yes! Because you are. I want you to be honest enough to admit it."

"Okay, so I admit it!" Jim finally agreed. "All it proves is what we both said before. It's one thing to know superstition is foolish, but it's an entirely new ball game to convince ourselves that it's true."

"Fine! Now that you've admitted it, there's something else I'm wondering about."

"What's that?" he asked.

"Well, I wonder how many other people have gotten swamped in the same spot with the monument getting the blame for their disappearance."

"Plenty, I'll bet."

"I'll bet you're right," she agreed, "if the breaker was as big as the one that hit us."

"One thing's for sure," Jim said, "if we ever sail through that place again we'll give it a wide berth."

"Hey, Jim!" There was a note of fear in Claudine's voice.

"What?"

"We've been so busy talking I never noticed. We're

not making any headway!"

"Of course we are."

"We are not!" she insisted. "We've been in the same spot for the past thirty minutes. Look for yourself. There's the bell buoy. Either it's moving as fast as we are or we're standing still."

"Bell buoys can't move. They're moored to the bottom of the ocean."

"I know that," she said impatiently.

Studying the buoy, Jim realized Claudine was right. "Wait a minute! Stop rowing."

"See! We're drifting toward the island."

"You're right, Claud! Come on! Let's put our backs to these oars!"

After ten minutes of hard rowing they hadn't moved any closer to the bell buoy. "Throw the anchor overboard," Jim ordered.

Claudine moved quickly into the bow and dropped the anchor into the water. She watched the line play out of the boat. It became taught. It stopped the backward motion of the dory with a jerk sending Claudine sprawling into the bottom of the boat.

No more than a few seconds later the dory began drifting again. "My God! The anchor line broke!" Claudine cried out.

"Grab your oars! Maybe we can hold her!" Jim shouted.

"What good is that going to do? We can't stay here for the rest of our lives!"

"We must be in an undertow. Sure, that's what it is. An undertow!" The discovery calmed Jim's nerves. "Now I see it. That's what caused the breaker. The undertow rushing against the swells!"

"Terrific! I'm glad to see your discovery has you all excited. Now all we have to do is live to tell about it!"

Jim suggested they row across the undertow instead of against it. "That way we might find an eddy that will carry us back toward home."

Claudine agreed and they began to row in an easterly direction across the current. It didn't take them long to realize that if they continued they would be carried out to sea even further.

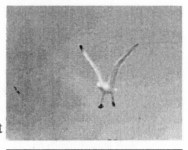

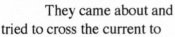
*A SEAGULL COMING IN
FOR AN ATTACK*

They came about and tried to cross the current to the west. Regardless of the winds help they were now being carried toward the island. They were within a mile of the monument and nearly exhausted. They agreed they should try to make a landing.

"And what about the current? Nobody, I mean nobody, ever said anything to me before about undertows or currents this far from shore."

"Don't think about it," Jim cautioned. "Just keep rowing. Once we get the boat beached we'll have plenty of time to think about it."

A hundred yards from the island Jim told Claudine to stop rowing. The boat stood near-motionless. The island blocked the wind and there was no longer any current.

They sat wide-eyed with amazement and observed the panorama before them. From the mainland the island appeared small. Even from the plane they didn't get a true picture of its size.

"Well, there it is," Jim said with a hushed voice.

"Yup, there it is all right." Claudine resigned to their predicament.

"Big, isn't it?" Jim said in awe.

"It sure is. I had no idea it was this big."

"Yeah, I know, and even from here you can tell it's bigger than the lighthouse!"

While Jim was talking a lone seagull turned in the air and began a steep glide toward them. The closer it got the faster it flew. They didn't notice the gull until an explosion of feathers and a loud screech preceded the slash of its bill at Jim's head. The attack startled them. They covered their heads with their arms.

A second gull took up where the first left off. Then another and another until there were hundreds of gulls diving at them. The noise grew from a mild nerve-bending aggravation to pandemonium.

Jim stood up in the boat and tried to beat off the gulls while Claudine rowed the remaining distance to shore. The gulls were so thick they looked like a large turbulent gray cloud. They blocked off the sun engulfing Jim and Claudine in the shade.

Jim and Claudine had to communicate with hand signals. In order to hear any words they had to shout into each other's ears.

As the boat hit the shore they both jumped out as quickly as they could. They rolled the dory bottomside up. They grabbed it by the bow and lifted it high enough for Jim to get his shoulders inside. Claudine placed an oar under the bow to form a lean-to protecting them from the gulls. Clam diggers used this method to shelter them from sudden showers on the clam flats.

Unable to protect themselves while they set up their fort, Jim had blood trickling down his face from a myriad of cuts on his head. The thickness of Claudine's hair provided her with better protection. She sustained only a few cuts.

It took about fifteen minutes for the nerve-shattering racket from the gulls to subside. The only sounds were those of the wind and water.

It amazed them that a scene of such frenzy changed so quickly to one of peace. Jim cleaned the blood from his face. "Boy, have we got ourselves into a mess!"

"You can say that again!"

Jim looked out over the water, then turning around, he studied the birds and what he could see of the island. "Let me think. Got to figure out how we're going to get out of this pickle. We could radio for help, but we don't have a radio. If we weren't on an island we could walk home. That's if we could even get out from under this boat."

"Oh, come on, Jim! Be serious!" Claudine scolded. "This is no joke!"

"That's for sure," he agreed. "But look at the bright side of this. Awhile ago we were fighting for our lives. Now we're nice and cozy, plus safe on dry land. Our trip was going to be a failure. At least we've succeeded in getting here. All we have to do is solve a few problems to get everything done we set out to do."

"You call that safe!" she protested.

"I said we had a few problems, didn't I? Now let's not panic! All I'm trying to do is give us a chance to get our wits together."

"Aren't you scared?" Claudine asked.

"What do you think?"

"I think you're scared."

"Well, you're right," he agreed. "I'm scared. And if we're going to get out of this mess we'd better keep our fears under control. It's always worked for us before. I don't see why it won't this time."

Claudine thought for a minute then with a little jerk of her head said, "Right! So let's figure out what we're going to do about the gulls first."

"Good idea," Jim said looking out at the mass of gulls. "Right now they're our biggest problem. They've completely calmed down, so I'm going to try to move up the beach without disturbing them."

Claudine began to pull the sail under the boat. "While you do that I'm going to try to make it a little more comfortable under here. This rocky beach is murder to sit on."

Jim eased himself out from under the boat staying flat on his belly. The gulls remained quiet. As he sat up a few noticed his movement and retreated with short quick steps with their bodies sideways and their heads turned to keep their eyes constantly on him.

He saw the seagulls everywhere; on the beach, in the

rocks, even in the thick undergrowth that covered most of the island. It was those in the bushes that looked strangest to him. He had never seen anything like it before.

He remained motionless in his sitting position until the gulls closest to him calmed down. He gradually brought himself to a kneeling stance. This time the seagulls began to call nervously and did not retreat. Jim remained rigid. The pain in his knees shot straight to his hips and he hardly dared to breathe. Again, the gulls quieted down within minutes.

He eased painfully to his feet. The birds studied him and Jim sensed their confusion. They withdrew a few feet and called anxiously to each other.

He moved his right foot forward. Nothing happened. Watching the seagulls intently he moved his left foot. Still quiet. He stood rigid. Only his eyes moved. Hundreds of little yellow eyes stared at him, never flinching, never looking at anything else but him.

He observed the gulls further up the beach and in the bushes. They were alert to danger, but nowhere near as tense as the ones closest to him. Again, he moved his right foot slowly and then his left. They still did not react. He stood still for a moment then repeated his action. Still no reaction.

He thought for a long time and finally decided to gamble and walk gradually toward the bushes and grass ahead of him. On his second step the whole scene exploded into a mass of white and gray thrashing wings. The crying of a thousand gulls in unison combined with the noise of their beating wings vibrated his body. The birds were all around him as they lifted off the ground.

Their wings engulfed him starting at his ankles and moving up his body. As he covered his head with his arms they moved up pass his shoulders. The noise was intense. Within an instant they were at head level.

Jim panicked. His ravaged nerves forced him to make an involuntary scream and his arms struck out indiscriminately in all directions. He turned and dove under the boat. He laid their for several minutes pressing his hands against his ears and gulping for air.

Baby Bum's Boat

Chapter IX

It took several minutes for Jim to recover from the shock of his experience. Claudine moved closer to him. Her hands shook as she reached out to check for cuts on his head. He flinched as she touched him. His eyes were wide with fear. He shook his head in an attempt to get his mind back to reality. He breathed a deep sigh and his body relaxed with relief.

"You all right now?" Claudine asked.

"I-I think so."

"What happened to you?"

"I really don't know. It isn't that the gulls scared me. I expected them to spook like that. It was almost like their bodies swallowed me up like that breaker. And the noise! It's the noise that got to me. The closer they got to my head the more my brain pounded. Finally the racket and the vibration took over my mind. I had to scream to keep it from completely getting to me."

Claudine shuddered. "Maybe it didn't scare you, but you sure scared me. I thought you'd lost your mind!"

"Well, I'm okay now, so let's get to figuring this thing out."

Claudine looked up at the dory's bottom. "A roof!" Her face lit up with excitement. "Some kind of roof. Like the boat is our roof right now. Sure! A portable roof is what we need!"

"An umbrella is a portable roof," Jim suggested.

"It sure is! And we can use some of the canvas from the sail!"

"We can unravel some of the anchor line for string to put them together. So all we need are some sticks and there are plenty of those on the beach."

"Good! I'll get some," she offered.

"Wait just a minute. You're not going out there!"

"Why not?" she demanded.

"Because."

"Because I'm a girl, right?"

"Okay, if you insist. Yes, because you're a girl," he admitted.

"If you don't stop being condescending, Jim Collins, I'm going to give you more problems than you have now!"

"Look, Claud, you've got to understand one thing. Our parents don't see things the way we do. As far as they're concerned, I should be responsible for you.

"If something happened to you while I stood by and did nothing to protect you they would never understand."

"They're not here!" she argued. "And besides, we're either going to get out of this thing together or not at all. So there's going to be nothing for you to explain one way or the other."

"Okay, okay, let's not fight over it. You go out one side and I'll go out the other. Stay flat on your stomach. I don't think that's as likely to spook them."

They were only able to gather a few sticks before the

gulls burst into action for the third time. They retreated quickly to their sanctuary.

"Well, that didn't work," she commented.

"Nope, it sure didn't. Do you think you can hold one end of this boat up?"

"I guess so," she said. "What are you thinking?"

"With the tide coming in we've got to move further from the water's edge. So, we might as well try to move the boat above the high-water mark.

"From there," Jim continued, "we should be able to reach enough driftwood without having to leave the shelter of the boat."

Claudine agreed. She placed her head and shoulders under the bow of the overturned dory and lifted. The oar holding up the bow dropped to the ground. Jim took it and stored it between the seats and bottom with the others. He crawled under the stern section and lifted it off the ground. With all of their strength they began to move. They looked like a strange four-legged monster as they labored the few yards up the beach.

Reaching their destination Jim lowered his end first. He got to Claudine as her knees began to buckle under the heavy load. Once the oar was back in place she dropped to the ground to rest.

Without a word he ducked out from under the boat into the flock of swarming seagulls. He ran to their original position, threw the sail over himself and dragged the broken mast and lines to the boat.

He dropped next to Claudine, exhausted. "It looks to me like we're stuck here for the night," he gasped.

"Oh, no! What about our folks! They'll be worried to death!"

"I know," he agreed. "But what choice have we got? It would be foolish to try to get back this late in the day. Especially after the trouble we've had already."

Claudine realized he was right. They set to work making their umbrellas. Having used the string they unraveled from the broken anchor line they made a sturdy frame with sticks and tied pieces of canvas to it. The finished product was crude, but good and rugged.

With that chore finished they started to make their shelter more comfortable. They used a heavy piece of driftwood instead of the oar under the bow. The shorter piece of driftwood gave them less headroom, but made it possible for them to close in the shelter on three sides with some of the canvas. They used the rest of the canvas to make the floor.

Jim stretched out on the floor to try it for comfort. "Could be worse! Now, if we only had some food all we'd have to do is sit and wait."

"Let's try the umbrellas," Claudine suggested.

"Okay," Jim agreed. "There's still plenty of daylight left. Let's go see if we can find a trail across the island."

Their exit from the shelter touched off the seagulls again. The striking of their beaks against the umbrellas sounded like a hail storm. The crude shields proved successful. It was hard on their nerves to see the gulls charging them, but none could touch them.

They moved into the bushes a short way, but the umbrellas were becoming a handicap. It was difficult to maneuver them through the heavy growth.

As they looked around to find a path they saw a boat hidden in the bushes. Stunned by what they saw they turned to each other with eyes and mouths wide open. It was Baby Bum's boat.

Jim signaled to retreat to the shelter. Once there they removed their maple staffs which had been secured to the bottom of the boat. They took positions on each side of the shelter. They looked intently for any sign of Baby Bum. Satisfied he wasn't nearby they ducked back under the boat. Quickly they changed the position of the canvas so they could see clearly on all sides.

Claudine was visibly shaken. "We're crazy! You know that, Jim? We're just plain nuts! Why can't we get our kicks like normal people? Oh, no! Not us! We go around

finding crazy people and dead people and looking for ghosts! Don't you agree that we're crazy?"

"Right now I'd say, yes. I'd settle for being anywhere but here. I'd even be happy is Miss Pringle's English class!"

"Yeah, I guess. Well, we'd better get to the job of survival," she suggested.

"Not yet, Claud. We'll wait until after dark in case he's watching us. You know, there's one thing for sure. If we get out of this mess I'm not going to wander any further than my living room for the next six months," he promised.

"Six months! I'm not going to stray more than two feet from my mother's arms, ever!"

"Hey! I just thought of something." Jim's face brightened. "If Baby Bum's on this island he can't be moving around much. The only time the gulls kicked up a storm was when we disturbed them!"

"You're right! Oh, come to think of it, he'd certainly know someone else is on the island the way we've had those gulls in the air every few minutes."

"Huh, that he would," Jim said frowning. Then his face brightened again. "Yeah, but by the same token, if he moves around we'll know it."

Jim looked out from under the boat. "I think it's dark enough now. Let's set up our obstacles. Move easy so we don't get the gulls going again."

They used the oars, driftwood and stones to build a circle of obstacles around their camp. They balanced rocks one on top of the other. They made trip-triggers with sticks. When they finished it would be impossible for anyone to get to them without being heard.

With their alarm system ready they settled themselves down for the night. It wasn't long before they had to face a new threat. Mosquitoes. Soon their buzzing sound was as annoying as the screech of the seagulls.

Jim was the first to complain. "This is lousy. We'll never make it through the night. My face feels like fire already."

"We've got to do something," Claudine agreed. "I've got a million bites on me at least! We're going to have to gamble, Jim. Let's drop the bow. We can use the canvas in place of screening."

"But we won't be able to see out," he objected.

"We'll have to depend on our ears," she argued. "We can't stand being chewed up like this all night!"

"Okay, let's do it. These mosquitoes are doing more damage to us than the gulls."

An hour after they finished sealing off their shelter the last of the mosquitoes were killed. Claudine cried out.

"What's the matter now?" Jim asked.

"Sand fleas, I think."

"Ouch! You're right," he agreed. "See if you can find the rope."

She reached toward the stern. "Here it is. Have you got your knife?"

"Yup." Jim cut four pieces of rope each long enough to tie their jeans at their ankles. He gave two to Claudine and kept the other two for himself.

"That should take care of them," he said.

Claudine settled herself down again. She started to think of home. "Our parents must be going out of their minds right about now."

"Just as long as we don't go out of ours," Jim advised. "In a way I'm glad you're here even though I wish you were home."

"How so?" she asked.

"Well, I'd sure hate to be here alone. I don't see how I could survive this without your help."

"Neither could I."

"Are you cold?" he asked.

"No."

"You're shaking all over."

"I'm scared."

"Oh! Well, so am I," he whispered. "Try not to worry about it. I've been thinking and if Baby Bum shows up here he couldn't do a thing to us without first rolling the boat over. Well, by the time he did all that we'd have both of his legs broken with our staffs.

"All we have to do is stay awake and listen. If we do, we've got all the advantages."

"I know all that, but I'm still scared," she confessed. "We'd better be quiet. It's hard enough to hear as it is."

"It's better we keep talking and stay awake than not and fall asleep."

"I suppose," she agreed.

Jim stared into the dark. "Listen to the gulls. Don't they ever shut up?"

"The waves are making almost as much noise," she complained.

"Weird, isn't it?" Jim thought out loud. "You'd think it would be so quiet out here that you could hear a pin drop."

"I know." she said. "I think it's as noisy here as in the city."

"Why don't you try to sleep. If I get drowsy I'll wake you up then you can guard for awhile."

"Okay." she said.

Less than an hour later Claudine asked, " Are you awake?"

"Yup. Can't you sleep?"

"No, I keep thinking I hear all kinds of strange noises."

"I know. Me, too. I've just about jumped out of my skin a hundred times."

"I wonder what time it is?" she asked.

"I don't know. But I can remember one time when I had the measles and couldn't sleep. It felt like the night lasted a week. Let's try to relax," he suggested. "Don't even think about time. Try to think of what Baby Bum could do to us and ways of keeping him from doing it."

"Is that your idea of relaxing!" Claudine was surprised by his suggestion.

"No, it's my idea of how to make time pass, plus figure how to survive."

"Sounds more like make-believe to me."

"There's nothing wrong with make-believe if it helps us to get out of this mess," Jim advised.

"Yeah. I guess you've got a good point there. I sure wish I could get a look outside."

"The place would be full of mosquitoes again if we did," Jim warned.

"I know! I can pull the plug out of the bottom." Claudine moved her hand around until she found it. Having removed the plug she changed her position until she got her eye lined up with the opening.

"See anything?"

"No, nothing. Look for yourself. It's as black as pitch out there."

Jim worked himself into position. "Yeah, you're right. It's...Wow! Lightning! We're going to have a storm!"

"Why not a thunderstorm?" Claudine said angrily. "We've had everything else. All we need now is an earthquake and a tital wave!"

"Shhhh," Jim warned. "Don't say it. You'll make it happen."

"We won't be able to hear anything," she complained. "A freight train could pass over us without our being able to hear it."

"Same plan, Claud. If he lifts this boat we smash his legs."

"You're right," she agreed. "Nothing's changed. There's only one thing, though. Why do I get the feeling I'm lying in a coffin?"

"It does kind of feel that way, doesn't it? Or at least what I suppose it must feel like. Of course, in a coffin we'd be holding flowers instead of these clubs!"

"Thanks for the cheerful thought," she said.

"You're welcome," he joked. "I'm always pleased to cheer up a friend."

The rain began. The downpour hit the boat drowning out all other sounds. Fortunately for them the dory made a watertight refuge. The storm raged on for several hours. They really had no idea of exactly how long it lasted because they had lost tack of time. To them daylight should've come hours before. Every time they pulled the plug from the bottom they found that it was still night.

They could feel every stone that made up the floor of their shelter dig into their bodies. Although it was too dark to see they never closed their eyes. At any moment Baby Bum could be on the attack.

"Isn't the night ever going to end?" Jim complained.

Claudine hushed him. "Listen!"

"What?" he asked in a whisper.

"The gulls are starting up again."

"Yeah, they are, aren't they! There' something different about the noise, though. Do you hear a difference? The noise is increasing little by little instead of a big explosion like before."

"So what? It still means Baby Bum is on the prowl out there!"

"Yeah, I know. You be ready on your side. I'm ready on mine. Let's both stay calm now. This is no time for panic. Okay?"

"Okay, Jim. We zapped him before and if we have to, we'll do it again!"

Suddenly Claudine's body stiffened with a jerk. She made a sound as if she was hit in the stomach.

Jim flinched. "What's the matter!" he cried out.

"I just thought of another way Baby Bum could get us out of here."

"How? Dig a tunnel?"

"He could set the boat on fire and burn us out like we did to him!"

Proof

Chapter X

Jim and Claudine lay in the blackness of their shelter ready for an attack by Baby Bum. They listened intently with their muscles taut and ready to spring into action.

The noise of the gulls intensified. "He must be getting closer!" Jim said.

Claudine tipped her head a little to one side. There was something different about the sound of the seagulls. She turned her head in the other direction thinking her other ear might be able to detect the variance.

"Pull the plug," Jim whispered. "See if you can see anything."

She reached up in the dark and removed it. Light came through the hole. "It's morning!" she shouted with joy.

"Quiet!" he warned. "Can you see anything else?"

"Yes, the gulls are all going in the same direction!"

"They're what?"

"All going in the same direction. See for yourself."

Claudine moved over so Jim could look. "They sure are! That's what they're doing all right. Huh, that sure is strange. We can't gamble on staying under here any longer. Help me get the canvas out of the way."

They had the canvas stored. Peeking out through the narrow space between the gunnel and the ground they couldn't see any sign of Baby Bum.

Jim outlined his plan to Claudine. "I'm going to crouch near the center of the boat. I'll put my staff at my feet then I'll grab the gunnel with both hands. When I give you the signal I'll lift with all my might and roll the boat over behind us. If he's on that side he'll have to jump out of the way because the boat will be coming at him. As soon as it rolls out of my way I'll dive for my staff while you come out swinging with yours."

Claudine moved to one side so Jim could get set. "I'm ready," she told him.

"Okay, so am I. Ready? Now!" he screamed, straining every muscle in his body as he lifted the boat away. Immediately he bent over and grabbed his staff. He was ready for the attack.

At the same time Claudine shot by him a few feet. She spun around in her tracks ready to protect Jim's back. They looked quickly in all directions and there was no sign of Baby Bum. They looked at the sky. It was bright orange. All the seagulls they could see where flying counterclockwise anywhere from one hundred to two hundred feet in the air forming a circle around the island.

"What on earth do you make of that?" Jim asked.

"It looks like some kind of ritual, doesn't it?"

Jim observed the spectacle. He tried to understand the seagulls' behavior and then his face brightened. "It's the sun," he said excitedly. "As the sun comes up their calls get more and more intense."

As the sun broke the horizon the gulls broke their formation. Their calls became more relaxed until they noticed Jim and Claudine. Without warning they charged down on them. They grabbed their umbrellas as fast as they could, barely making it before the gulls struck. Again, the sound was like heavy hailstones as their beaks hit the canvas.

Jim put his head under Claudine's umbrella. "I don't see any rescue boats out there," he shouted over the screeching of the seagulls. "Let's go inland to see if we can find some berries or something to eat."

After walking into the brush a short way they found an abundance of berries. They put down their umbrellas and ate until they were full. Some of the bushes were as much as ten feet high which prevented the gulls from attacking.

With their appetites satisfied they began to work their way inland. They struggled though the brush and up a gentle slope toward the monument. To keep from losing their direction they kept their eye on the only visible part of the monument, the top.

After traveling about a half-mile the land started on a downward slope and the monument was no longer in view. They descended into a valley. The further they went the

HEAVY UNDERGROWTH BY THE POND ON MONUMENT ISLAND

thicker the brush became. It tore at their skin and clothing with every step.

Having found a place to sit they decided to rest. "What do you think?" Jim asked thoughtfully.

Claudine wiped her face with the sleeve of her jacket. "I'm beginning to think we made a mistake. That's what I think."

"Me, too."

"Maybe we should have followed the shore," she suggested.

"Yeah, well I'm beginning to think so. Even if it is a lot longer I'll bet it will be a lot quicker."

"Why don't we keep going a little while longer considering we've come this far. If it doesn't get any better we'll head back to the boat."

"Okay by me," he agreed. "We're bound to come out of this brush soon, I hope."

They got to their feet and began to push through the brush again. Within two hundred yards the brush came to an end only to find a large pond blocking their way. The water in the pond was dark and had a foul odor.

"I don't like this place." Claudine said nervously.

"I don't, either." Jim pointed to the upper end of the pond. "Maybe we can cross over there. It's a lot narrower. Come on, you follow me."

He had gone but a short way when the ground became soft. Suddenly he sank to his knees. As he struggled to get free he sank deeper. "It's quicksand!" he shouted. "Here, grab the end of my staff."

Claudine pulled on the staff and in a minute Jim was back on solid ground. "I sure am getting sick of all this," he complained. "Isn't anything going to go right for us? All we did is start out on a little boat ride. It should have taken us four hours at the most. Now here we are on the second day still stuck in the mud!"

"Take it easy, Jim!"

"Take it easy? This lousy trip is jinxed!"

"Oh, come on now," she scolded. "Sit down for a minute. It's time we took one of our 'don't-push-the-panic-button' breaks."

"Yeah, you're right," he said disappointed with himself. "I think we'd better get back to the boat and take our chances with the ocean."

"You're not giving up are you?" she asked, surprised by his mood.

"I don't know. Let's get back to the boat. We'll decide what to do when we get there."

Walking for almost an hour Jim told Claudine to sit down. He looked around for several minutes and then told her they were lost. "We should have been out of here by now."

Claudine agreed. She said she wasn't worried. "After all, this is an island. We're bound to come out on shore sooner or later."

Jim looked up at her. "You amaze me. You're as calm as if we were on a Sunday School picnic or something!"

"No, I'm not," she argued. "It's just that I've been so scared I don't think there's anything left in me to scare." She wasn't looking at him when she spoke. Something else had her attention. "Look over there," she said with her voice becoming a whisper.

"Where?" he asked.

"Right there," she said as she pointed to the spot. "Just a few feet behind you. Is that what I think it is?"

Jim turned and peered at the ground. Then he saw it. "Oh my God! It's a skeleton!" He stood up and walked to it. He poked around it with his staff clearing away some of the sticks and leaves partially covering it. He turned toward Claudine. "Well, we know that at least one person has died on this island and that's for sure!"

"Come on over here, Claud. Let's see if we can find any clues to lead us to who it is."

"I don't want to touch that thing," she protested.

"We've got to," he argued. "There's no way we could

ever find this spot again. He picked up a small stick and carefully began to clear the area. Eventually they found a belt buckle, the blade of a knife and a rusted pistol. "We're going to take the skull along with the rest of this stuff," he told Claudine. "Maybe it will help identify him."

Claudine studied the skeleton. "I wonder how he died."

"From panic, I bet. Look at the skull. See how the jawbone is set. Like he must have been screaming or yelling."

"That's right, it is, isn't it! And the gun. From where we found it he must've had it in his hand."

"Okay, so when he died he must have been in fear for his life," Jim observed. "Let's see what else we can figure out."

"He was right about fearing for his life," she said. "I mean he is dead, so he had to be right!"

"Not necessarily."

"Well, he is dead, isn't he?"

"Sure, but that doesn't prove somebody or something killed him," Jim insisted. "Look at his bones. None of them are broken. He's lying face down like he fell and the way the skull is twisted it looks like he was trying to see something behind him."

Claudine moved a few steps to get a better view. She studied the skeleton for another minute. "Could be, I suppose. Now that you mention it, the position of the skeleton makes me think of a cat running up a tree and looking back to see if he's safe."

"You're right!" He bent over for a better look. "Except for the legs. Something isn't quite right about the legs." He pointed to the right leg. "Every part of the skeleton looks like it's trying to get away from something except the right leg."

Claudine became engrossed in the puzzle. She walked around the legs of the skeleton. She frowned, "I can't figure out what to make of this mound of earth. It looks like a half-moon. He must have pushed it that way with his foot."

Jim observed the mound that formed an arc around the left foot. "I think you're right. It seems that every part of him was struggling except his right leg! I wonder why?"

Claudine's face brightened. "I think I've got it."

"You do?"

"Yeah. Listen carefully. Hear the wind blowing through the brush and the sound of the gulls?"

"Yeah, what about it?"

"Well, picture yourself scared out of your wits. Now what does the wind and the gulls sound like?"

"Yeah! I think I see what you mean! It sounds like all of the evil things on earth crying in pain. Sure, just like the Bible says, 'the wailing and gnashing of teeth'. I'll bet to a superstitious man it would sound like the devil and his legions coming after him!"

"Like a whole bunch of spooks," Claudine added.

"Okay, I agree with you, but I still don't see where you're going with this."

"You're standing on it," she said.

"Standing on what?"

"On the best clue of all," she said.

"You sure you're not spooked yourself? I don't see anything."

"The vines. Look at the vines." She bent over and picked one up. "Try to break it. I'll bet you can't."

"I swear, Claud, I don't know what you're talking about."

"Well, look for yourself," she said. "From everything we've figured out so far we can tell he was in panic and then he fell. After falling he thrashed around on the ground and died.

Now the way I see it, his right leg got tangled in one of these vines. He thought something had caught him by the leg. He was so scared he kept fighting until there was no life left in him."

Jim looked at Claudine, and then at the vines and skeleton.

He put his hand to his chin and stood there thoughtfully for a couple minutes. "You know, I wouldn't be a bit surprised if you were right."

"Okay, I got that figured out. Now you figure out how we're going to get out of here."

Jim nodded in agreement. He looked through the brush trying to spot the top of the monument. He couldn't. He studied the slope of the land then looked up and checked the position of the sun.

"I think we should keep the sun to our left," he said. "That should keep us in the right direction. In any event, it will keep us from traveling in circles."

Claudine took Jim's jacket and spread it on the ground. She placed the skull, knife, gun and buckle in it. She tied it into a bundle and Jim attached it to his belt.

He held his umbrella in front of him to force a path through the brush. Claudine followed close behind him and acted as a rear guard. After going about twenty yards they stopped to rest. "This is impossible. I hope we don't have much further to go or we might not get out of here before dark."

Claudine nodded her head. They dropped to the ground, weary of fighting branches. For the first time they rested without saying a word to each other. Their arms hung limply at their sides and their heads drooped. Sweat ran down their faces and their lungs struggled for air.

A few more minutes passed. Jim lifted his head toward Claudine, "My God, I'm thirsty."

When she heard him speak she looked up. Her eyes were dull with their usual sparkle gone. She nodded her head in recognition and then let it drop again.

Claudine suggested they eat more berries. "They should help to quench our thirst a little."

"Okay, but we've got to figure out something better than this. I mean at this rate if we do get out of here we won't have any strength left for the trip home."

"Trip home! What if we run into Baby Bum. Right

now I don't think I could get to my feet, leave alone fight him."

"That's for sure," he agreed. "I wonder how far we've come?" I mean we can't have much farther to go. It's taken us twice as long trying to get out as it took us to get in!"

"Sure, but we were fresh when we went in. Now we're beat."

Jim looked at his umbrella. Let's take these things apart. Maybe we can do better without them."

"What about the gulls?"

"They can't get us right now," he said. "Once we're close enough to the beach we'll put them back together."

"Yeah, we can do that all right, but it's the umbrellas that keep the branches from really tearing us to pieces."

"Yeah, and it's taking all of our strength to push them through this mess," he argued. "Now look down here." He bent low to the ground and pointed to the base of the bushes. "See, it's almost like a tunnel. If we crawl on our hands and knees we should make better time without using as much energy."

"And most likely get lost again," she said. "But I suppose anything is better than what we've been doing."

Jim shrugged his shoulders. "Well, it's worth a try, anyway."

They took the umbrellas apart, rolled the sticks inside the canvas and tied the bundle with the string.

With their staffs in one hand and the umbrellas in the other they began to crawl through the brush. Jim had the worst of it. The bundle holding the skull and belongings of the skeleton kept getting in the way of his knees as he tried to crawl.

They took another break and Claudine tied the bundle so that it hung from Jim's chest. They were now able to move more quickly through the brush covering the next two hundred yards in a fraction of the time.

They moved on until they came to another patch of blackberries. As they ate Claudine noticed there were more gulls overhead and the bushes weren't as thick.

Jim agreed and stopped picking berries. He looked around for a moment and asked, "Is this where we picked berries this morning?"

For the first time in quite awhile Claudine's face showed a smile. "It is! I know it is! There's the broken branches where we passed earlier."

Jim spun around and looked. "Sure enough, there it is," he shouted as he threw his arms up and jumped.

"We've made it! We've made it!" she yelled along with him. She reached out, took him by the arm and they started to dance.

"Hold it! Hold it!" he shouted. "These bushes are going to make spaghetti out of us if we don't stop."

Claudine headed for the path they had broken through that morning. Jim shouted for her to stop. "Have you forgotten about Baby Bum and the gulls?" he warned.

As he caught her he signaled her to be quiet and to get down. "We'll move to the very edge of the bushes," he said quietly. "Close enough so we can see our boat. After we make sure there's no Baby Bum around we'll duck under the boat and try to figure out what we'll do next."

No Inscription

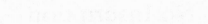

Chapter XI

Jim crawled only a few feet at a time. He looked through the brush as far as he could in all directions. Claudine watched behind him. If Baby Bum was nearby Jim was going to make sure they saw him first.

They finally saw their boat. "Oh, no!" Jim moaned. "I forgot! We rolled the boat over when we got out. Now we've got no place to hide from the gulls."

"We can put the umbrellas back together," Claudine suggested.

"We're going to have to," he said as he started to untie the strings holding his umbrella together.

"Any sign of Baby Bum?" she asked.

"There's no sign of anything. Where the devil is the Coast Guard? Somebody should be out there looking for us!"

"Maybe they've come and gone."

"If they saw our boat they wouldn't leave without finding us."

"They wouldn't, huh," she argued. "What about the guy we found? Nobody rescued him."

"That's different."

"What's different about it?" she insisted.

"He most likely got lost before there was any Coast Guard around these parts."

"Maybe, maybe not," Claudine said.

Jim held up his umbrella. "Okay, mine's ready."

"Mine will be in a minute."

While she finished Jim took another look around. As they moved toward the boat the gulls took to the air ready to battle their familiar intruders.

It took only a few minutes for them to set the shelter up and this time they arranged it so they had a better view of the area around them.

They rested on the canvas under the boat for fifteen minutes. It didn't appear anything had been disturbed while they were gone.

"I'd guess it's about noontime, maybe earlier. What do you think?" Claudine asked.

Jim looked up at the sun then at the water. As he turned to Claudine he said, "It was low tide at eight in the morning yesterday. Judging by where the water is on the beach, I'd say it's about eleven."

"Okay," she agreed. "Well, there are no boats in sight and we've got at least eight hours of daylight left, so I think we might as well follow the shore and get a look at the monument."

"I'm with you," he said enthusiastically. "We should be back here in plenty of time." He looked out over the water. "If we don't see a boat by four o'clock we'll make a try at rowing to the mainland.

"The way I see it, the tide will be going out instead of coming in, like yesterday. That means the current should help us instead of drive us out to sea."

"That makes sense to me," she said.

Jim made two coils of rope using the mast stays and anchor line. He placed one over his shoulder and gave the other to Claudine. "We might need these along the ledges," he said. He took another look around. "Well, this is it! Let's go!"

They crawled out from under the boat, lifted their umbrellas and started toward the rock ledges that made up most of the shore. This time the gulls were able to carry on their attack without the tall bushes getting in their way.

Claudine moved over the ledges with ease. She soon had a long lead on Jim. As she looked back she saw he was trailing behind, so she stopped and waited.

"Take it easy, will you?" Jim shouted.

"What's the matter? Can't keep up?" she teased.

"These rocks are very slippery," he argued. "The way you're going we could have an accident, so slow down. Besides, we've still got Baby Bum to worry about, so let's stay together."

"Okay, I'll try to take it easy on you." Claudine was still smiling.

By now most of the gulls had tired. There were still a great many swooping down at them, but the noise was less deafening.

Claudine was still in the lead as they reached the easterly end of the island. Once around the point they would be on the ocean side with the mainland out of view.

She stopped suddenly. She turned to Jim and pointed out to sea excitedly. A few miles from shore was a lobster boat. As soon as Jim saw it he ran past Claudine toward the point waving his staff in the air.

In his excitement he slipped on the rocks and fell off the ledge into the water. Claudine screamed, dropped her umbrella, took the rope from her shoulder and ran to help him. In her haste she almost fell as well.

She saw Jim trying to stay afloat in a mass of churning water. He fell into a pool the size of a basketball court.

THE OPENING TO THE SMALL POOL WHERE JIM ALMOST DROWNED

There was an opening in the ten-foot wall the width of a garage door at one end.

Every time a wave reached the rocky shore the water piled up in the entrance several feet higher than the water in the pool. In the next instant the water sped through the opening with great force. The turbulence carried Jim back and forth across the pool threatening to drag him out to sea.

Claudine threw one end of her rope to him. She missed. She pulled it back and tried again. She missed again. The third time he got a hold of it and tied it around his waist.

She started to pull him in, straining every muscle. Her feet slipped. She almost went over the edge a second time. She scrambled back to her feet and looked for a place to anchor the rope. Having spotted an outcrop of rock nearby she tied the rope to it.

Jim was able to get to the bottom edge of the ledge. With his free hand he threw his rope to Claudine. She tied it to the rocks with the other end around her waist. She was now protected from falling into the pool. She dropped what was left of Jim's rope to him. He tied it to his waist. Claudine was now able to pull him up over the ledge while he climbed the other rope to safety.

The moment he was safe Claudine grabbed her umbrella and put it over the both of them. While the rescue was going on she was not able to protect herself from the gulls. Blood flowed over her forehead and face.

Jim tore off a piece of his wet tee-shirt and used it to clean her cuts. "You wouldn't believe how awful you look," he laughed.

"Gee, thanks a bunch," she scolded. "Here I save your life and that's the thanks I get."

"Really, Claud, your head is full of bumps and your face is covered with scratches and mosquito bites."

"Well, you don't look any different," she argued.

"I know," he agreed. "We'd most likely scare anybody to death who happened to see us!"

When Jim fell into the water he managed to save his staff but lost his umbrella. Claudine thought it was going to be awkward with both of them having to use the same umbrella.

"Why do gulls always strike at our heads?"

Claudine looked puzzled. She thought for a minute then with a frown on her face she told him she didn't know.

"Because that's the only place they can hit us," he said. "You've seen swallows attack crows. Did you ever notice they dive at the crow from above then peck them on the head?"

"That's right! I never thought of it before, but why?"

"Well, think about it," he replied. "The gulls swoop down real close to our heads. The instant they're over us they drive their heads down and hit us with their beaks.

There's no other way they can do it. The only way they can strike is down. Now, if they tried to peck us any place else on our bodies their wings would hit us and they would crash. It's because of their wings that they can't strike us any other way. Watch," he said excitedly. "I'll hold my staff straight up and down so one end sticks up a couple of feet over my head and I'll bet the gulls can't hit me."

He stepped out from under the umbrella's protection and walked a few yards from Claudine. The gulls swooped to the attack striking the end of his staff rather than his head.

He walked back to Claudine. "See, I told you so."

"Terrific!" she shouted. "Now I can throw this awkward thing away."

"Go ahead." As he looked out to sea, he added, "Well, we missed that chance. That boat is gone now."

"There'll be others. Come on, let's get going. We've got a lot of time to make up."

"Okay," he agreed, "but no more running. We don't have far to go, so let's take it one step at a time.

"I'm not so sure there's no such thing as spooks," he continued. "It sure seems like something is fouling up our plans every few minutes."

"I'll buy that," she agreed.

Once they were around the point the monument came into view. They saw that it would be easy to get it from the shore. It stood a hundred yards inland from the rocky coast.

Jim took the lead. He walked slowly and stopped every few minutes. Every time he saw a possible hiding place where Baby Bum might be he approached it from one side and Claudine from the other.

Eventually they reached a good spot to move inland toward the monument. The bushes were in bunches with plenty of open space between them. The only obstacle was the waist-high grass. An army could hide in it, Jim thought.

They stopped a few feet from it. Jim studied the ground carefully then his graze moved up the walls of the monument until his head was tipped back as far as it could go. "Huge, isn't it?"

"I never thought it was so big," she agreed. "It doesn't make any sense to me at all," he said. "I mean, what's it doing here? Who built it, and why? And if it's intended as a marker for ship navigation why build it here when the shipping lanes are east of Wood Island?"

THE STONE TEEPEE

"I know, it's crazy! Look at the size of the boulder that forms the top. It's bigger than a garage! Now how could anything get a rock the size of that up there? Do you suppose it was built like the pyramids?" she wondered.

"I doubt it."

"It scares me, Jim" she confessed.

"You and me, both," he agreed. "There's something not of this world about this place. Something very strange. I think we should scram as quick as our legs will take us out of here."

They stood motionless and stared at the monument. The clouds drifting past the top made it look as if it was moving toward them. They were silent. Claudine took a step backward. Jim half turned as if he was about to run from the wicked place.

Claudine grabbed Jim's arm. He spun around toward her at the feel of her touch. "I'm cold," she said.

"Come on, let's get out of here," he said.

"No!" she cried out.

"I don't want to be responsible if something goes wrong," he insisted.

"If something goes wrong it's not going to make any difference," she argued.

"You mean you still want to go on with this!" Jim shook his head in disbelief.

"No, I don't," she said. "But if we don't go up there we won't be able to live with ourselves. Besides, you're not about to walk away from here now that we're this close."

"You're right, you know. Maybe there's something wrong with us. Maybe we're even crazy, but one way or the other we've got to figure this thing out."

"Okay, now that that's settled let's get up there and get this over with," she said. "You get about ten feet to my right. We'll move through the grass staying even with each other."

They moved in keeping their staffs high enough to keep the gulls from hitting, yet low enough to strike if they had to.

Every twenty feet or so they stopped, listened intently and always looked in all directions for possible danger. They were within spitting distance from the base. Jim stopped. He signaled Claudine with his hand to do the same.

The base of the monument was clearly visible. The earth formed a mound that extended ten feet from all sides giving it the appearance of setting on a small plateau. The grass on the mound was short in contrast to the rest of the area.

Jim looked for some kind of plaque or inscription that explained the origin of the monument, but there was nothing there.

He moved closer to Claudine and motioned her to move toward the front. They were careful to keep the distance between them and the monument. He continued to look for some kind of documentation, but there was still nothing to be seen.

They reversed their direction and walked to where

Jim had stopped originally. They started to inspect the other side. There was no sign made by civilized man on any part of the monument that they could see.

They moved opposite the entrance. There was no brass plaque or inscription there either. "Unreal!" Jim whispered. "A monument higher than a five-story building with no identification on it!"

"It's crazy," she agreed. "Civilized people don't build things like this without some kind of documentation."

"Civilized people? Why the cavemen even scribbled things on the walls of their caves! Okay, stay a couple of feet to my left." Jim stepped forward one slow step after the other. They both stared at the entrance trying to see inside.

It wasn't long before they stood close enough to be able to touch it with the end of their staffs. Claudine stood to the left side of the entrance, Jim to the right. The gulls broke off their attacks. They could no longer swoop down on them without running into the monument.

"Will you look at the thickness of that wall!" Jim said.

"It must be four feet thick!" Claudine said.

"Just about. It's almost as thick as the entrance is high."

"Are you ready?" He took the final steps to the opening. "I'm going to try to see inside."

Two Tenants

Chapter XII

Jim placed his hands against the monument one on each side of the entrance. He braced himself as if he was scared of being sucked into it.

As he leaned forward he peered inside. It was too dark to see anything. He moved to one side so his body would not block the light.

Gradually his eyes adjusted to the darkness. He still couldn't see a thing. As he turned toward Claudine, he shouted, "There's nothing in there!"

"Are you sure?"

"Not that I can see. Come here. You guard the entrance. I'm going to go in. I sure wish we hadn't lost our flashlight," he complained as he moved within the wall of stone.

Claudine took her position at the opening. "Aren't you going in the rest of the way?"

"In a minute. I want my eyes to adjust to the darkness." He took the final step to the end of the entrance tunnel. He stood still and listened. "There's a strange odor in here."

"Do you see anything?"

"Not yet," he answered. "Step inside the wall. I don't want you getting zapped from behind."

"Okay."

"Never mind," he called. "You better come over here with me. You're blocking the light."

Claudine followed his instructions. "Okay, now here's what we're going to do," he said. "I'm going to step inside and stand to the left of the entrance while you do the same only you stand to the right.

"We'll both stay put until our eyes get used to the darkness. Okay? Now!"

On Jim's signal they moved inside. The only light was what came from the narrow tunnel through the four-foot wall.

"Can you see anything, Claud?"

"Nothing, yet. How about you?"

"Nothing. I don't think there's a thing in here!"

"I wonder what that odor is?" she asked.

"I don't know. It isn't like anything I've ever smelled before. Can you see yet?"

"Some. I don't see anything on this side."

"Nothing over here, either. Wait a minute! What's over there?" He took a couple of steps away from Claudine to his left. He raised his staff in front of him. Bending over he strained to see better.

Suddenly his vision focused on a pair of eyes which were staring back at him. As his mind grasped what his eyes had seen the skin starting at his neck then traveling to his feet felt like a thousand spiders were crawling over it. He bolted backwards bumping into Claudine.

"What is it!" she cried out.

He was unable to answer. His stomach muscles were

ENTRANCE TO THE MONUMENT

in a fit causing air to rush in and out of his lungs. He was in a near crouch and held his arms extended in front of him with his staff ready to strike. Each muscle in his body acted independently of the others causing him to shake and jerk out of control.

"What is it!" Claudine screamed.

Jim stood up. His chest heaved as he gulped air. His body was covered with sweat. He leaned against the wall for support. After a few moments he recovered enough to speak. "There's someone looking at us! He's sitting on the floor against the wall over there!"

"There is!" she said frightened. "Why doesn't he do

something?"

"I don't know," he replied nervously. "You go that way. I'll go to the left."

They moved to within a few feet from the sitting figure. "That's close enough," Jim ordered. He reached out with the end of his staff and jolted the body. "Whatever it is, it's dead," he said with relief.

"Don't touch it until you're positive," Claudine warned.

"Don't worry, I won't." Jim poked the body again.

Claudine moved in closer. "My God! It's Baby Bum!" she screamed.

"Hah, so it is! So this is what happened to him. No wonder they couldn't find him."

"He didn't scare you much did he, Jim?" she laughed with relief.

"Never mind," he said. "It wasn't a bit funny. You wouldn't have acted any different if it had been you who saw those eyes staring at you."

I thought you were going to die there for a minute," she teased.

"Don't you ever dare tell anyone about that," he warned.

"Okay, I promise. What do you say we get out of here. My head feels real strange."

"So does mine," he said. "The air must be dead in here or something."

"What about Baby Bum?" she asked.

"He's not going anywhere. Let the cops come get him out."

"That's okay with me," she said as she started for the entrance.

Jim reached out and grabbed her by the arm. He spun her around to face him. "We did it!" he shouted joyfully. "We did it!"

"We sure did," she said as she turned toward the entrance again. "But let's save our celebrating until we're home."

"Please, please don't go."

"But you just said let's get out of here," Jim said.

"I didn't say that!" she cried with alarm.

"Come on, Claud! Stop kidding around!"

"Wait! Please, don't go."

"Cut it out, Claud! That's not funny!" he demanded.

"It's not me, I'm telling you!" She turned as she spoke and held onto Jim for support.

With their eyes opened as wide as their mouths they stared into the darkness; first along the floor then the walls. As they tipped their heads back they tried to see above them. The darkness above was complete.

Suddenly they were enveloped by a soft white light. It was now as bright as day inside the monument. Yet all they saw was the light. "Please don't be frightened," the gentle voice spoke. "I wish to do you no harm."

Jim and Claudine clutched on to each other. Jim tried to speak. Nothing but gasps of air passed his throat. Finally, Claudine managed to shutter, "Wh-wh-who are-are you?"

"I am the spirit of Squaw Sachem. Without you, I will have to spend eternity in the stone teepee. Unless you forgive me I will never be able to join the Great Spirit."

"For-forgive you for what?" Jim stammered.

"I am the one who cursed the river." Her soft voice filled the monument like a gentle puff of air. The Great Spirit has imprisoned me here until I have been forgiven by one of your race. Even though one of your race had done me a grievous wrong I returned hate with hate. I violated nature by making the river a stream of death when it had been a source of life. Only if you can find enough love in your heart to forgive me and I, in turn, will forgive your race, will my spirit be free."

Her soft voice had a calming effect. Jim and Claudine relaxed a little. "I can't see you," Claudine said.

"I am here," Squaw Sachem replied. "My spirit fills the teepee."

"Oh, I see. No, I don't see. I'm sorry, I mean, I understand," Claudine apologized.

"Do you mean to say that in over two hundred years, nobody would forgive you!" Jim asked.

"No one but the evil man who wanted to kill you has ever come in here. That is, until you came." she said.

"Did you kill him?" Claudine asked.

"He like the one you found were killed by the evil spirits they welcomed into their souls.

"All of nature's things live in harmony with Her. My people lived in harmony with nature and I sinned against Her. For that I have been punished severely. It is the nature of all life to survive, but it is the nature of all life to die as well. Only man knows he must die. Your people, instead of facing life and death with courage, waste their lives fearing death. Their minds become the lodges of evil things. My people knew this. They told your ancestors this was a place of evil spirits and if they entered here no one would ever see them again; not their bodies or their spirits. They wished me to suffer forever for the great wrong I had done. Forgive me so I may be free and I will give you the greatest gifts of all."

"Sure," Jim agreed. "If it's up to us, we're glad to be able to forgive you."

"This then I give you," the spirit of Squaw Sachem spoke. "That your souls will always be in harmony with nature and your minds will always be free of evil superstitions. There are no greater gifts than these for these are the Mother and Father of all that is good."

As she finished speaking the interior grew dark. "Jim, snap out of it!" Claudine shouted. "Come on, Jim. Let's get with it." She shook him violently.

"Huh! What's the matter?"

"It's time we got out of here," she insisted.

"Sure! Well, what are you waiting for? Let's go."

As they left the monument behind them, Jim asked, "Was that for real in there?"

"I don't know. My head felt so strange. And I didn't

think I'd ever get your attention again. I had to shake you for a full minute before you answered me."

"Hey, the gulls are gone!" he shouted in delight. Jim ran across the grass and leaped high into the air. Claudine did the same.

When they reached the shore Jim threw his staff as far as he could out over the water. "There!" he shouted with glee. "I won't need that thing anymore."

"Neither will I," Claudine shouted and threw hers out onto the waves.

"Come on, I'll race you back to the boat," she teased him.

Away they went over the rocks and ledges, skipping and jumping from one rock to the other. Claudine reached the point first. She let go with a rebel yell. As she looked back at Jim she pointed toward the little beach where they had been marooned.

"It's the Coast Guard," she shouted.

In less than a half-hour they were on board the Coast Guard cutter with their boat in tow.

The officer in command radioed the station and instructed them to telephone the police that Baby Bum's body was in the monument and to let Jim's and Claudine's parents know they were safe.

On the ride to the village they sat on the bow of the cutter and enjoyed the sun and the meal the crew had given them.

"You sure we weren't dreaming?" Jim asked.

"I don't think so."

"Well, my head sure felt strange in there."

"Maybe," she said. "But how come the gulls are gone?"

Jim looked at Claudine affectionately. "Maybe, just maybe, someday we'll have the answers."

She returned his look then blushed a little. "Why are you looking at me that way?"

"I want to ask you something."

"What?"

"Will you marry me?"

"Oh, Jim, we're just kids!"

"Oh, yeah?"